EV.

Winslow Swan

Published by Winslow Swan
Amazon Kindle Edition

Copyright 2018 by Winslow Swan

Other Works by this Author
The Convincer
Click (a tale of revenge)
Toppling Over The Edge
The Suicide Killers: The First Jake Rhodes Mystery
More Stories To Read To The Thing Under The Bed
Feather Brained
Creepy Short Stories To Read To
The Creature In The Closet
The Hitchcock Killer: The Second
Jake Rhodes Mystery
Do Not Read This Book
No One Is Afraid Of Monsters Anymore
(and other stories to read to the Thing
under the bed) Audio book Edition

This ebook is licensed for your personal enjoyment only. This ebook may not be re-sold or given away to other people. If you would like to share this book with another person, please purchase an additional copy for each recipient. If you are reading this book and did not purchase it, or it was not purchased for your use only, then please return to Amazon.com and purchase your own copy. Thank you for respecting the hard work of this author

A WORD FROM THE AUTHOR

The inspiration for this particular story came to me while watching a marathon of horror movies from the sixties, mostly starring my favorite actor, Vincent Price. Apparently, haunted houses were very big during the turbulent times of that period in this country's history. There was of course the original "House on Haunted Hill" and "Thirteen Ghosts" (which by the way I not only enjoy the originals but also the very clever remakes of both films) as well as an assortment of others. These other films if you care to look them up were "The Legend of Hell House", "The Old Dark House", and others too numerous to mention.

The one thing that I noticed is that there is always an underlying factor of death which precedes any good haunted house story. With that in mind, I wanted to create something that for the most part had not been done before. I hope that you will agree.

I must also warn you, dear reader, that the following story contains many graphic scenes of a sexual nature. If your sensibilities run to a more moral type of writing, I suggest that you read no further. I realized while writing and editing this particular book that I had not written such sexual scenes since writing my first novel "The Convincer" way back in 2007. That particular tome took almost four years to finally finish and publish and was a great relief to me when I was able to exorcise the main character from my fevered mind.

This story actually haunted me and was partially derived from a rather nasty nightmare that left me bathed in a cold sweat one night. I at least had the sense to write out what I could remember of the dream, filling in the blank spaces with my own imagination.

I sincerely hope that this particular book will give you a certain amount of chills as you lay in your safe and warm bed with expectations of horror and that it also gives you the nightmares that readers of horror and suspense so richly deserve. If truth be known, that is the exact reason that I have read and watched this type of entertainment.

Please be aware also that everything that happens within is from my own imagination. So with that in mind, please remember that the title reflects a belief that I have had since coming into this world. There is evil within all of us, a capacity that was endowed to us to choose whether we act upon a situation or not. I sincerely believe that the majority overcomes this evil that tries so desperately to escape from our inner beings. Yet, by looking at the news on television or reading the paper or hearing the radio, we discover that there are those who choose the darker side of the mind. Some even relish it.

So now, bathe yourself in the soft glow of the bedside lamp as you pull the covers around you a little tighter. Check the corners of your bedroom for those shadows that seem to be a little darker than the surrounding area and proceed to read my little story of madness and mayhem.

Enjoy!

Prologue
April 17th, 1976

Professor Barry Hale had been driving throughout the night. Periodically he would glance into the rearview mirror, waiting for the flashing blue lights that would end his journey. He was positive that someone would have discovered the ghastly remains of the female student that he had left in his office only three hours ago. He adjusted the mirror slightly and looked at the image that reflected back at him, his eyes darting from the mirror to the winding road ahead of him.

The dark circles under his eyes had become more prevalent in the last week. His cheeks were sunken in as if he had been starving. His hair, usually immaculate and always coifed to perfection was wild and stringy not having been washed in over a week. While he was thin to the point of looking sickly, he had been in the best of health according to his doctor, but even he could see the changes that were now reflected in the mirror.

He repositioned the mirror to reflect the road behind him. A pair of headlights appeared from some road that he had passed and his hands tightened their grip on the steering wheel. Could this be the police car that he had been waiting for ever since he left the college campus?

The car stayed behind him at a respectful distance for about five miles before turning onto another side road. The professor breathed a sigh of relief as his hands relaxed the death hold on the steering wheel.

He wasn't exactly sure where he was going. There had been no plan made after the incident, which is what he was calling it for fear that he might have actually gone insane. All that he truly knew was that he had to get as far away from the campus as possible and away from the body of the girl whose entrails lay sprawled over his desk, a look of panic and terror forever frozen on the young face.

He glanced over at the passenger seat, a shiver running up his spine like an icy skeletal finger. The package that lay there seemed to pulse with an energy that filled the car as it went racing on into the night. He couldn't take his eyes off of the small thing wrapped in a blood soaked towel that he had managed to find in the small bathroom that was part of his office. He thought that the blood stains were even more hideous than the corpse of the young girl who was to be forever known as the victim of a heinous crime.

A professor of archeology, he had been teaching at the college for only three weeks, recently returned from a dig somewhere in the Amazon where someone had turned up an unknown temple, buried deep in the jungle for thousands of years. He had been one of the first scientists to arrive and had managed to catalog a number of items for return to some museum as long as the proper authorities had been notified.

When he had first seen the small stone lying on what appeared to be a sort of pulpit deep within the catacombs of the dig, he could have sworn that it had pulsated with a light that seemed to hold him fast. He had convinced himself that it was only his mind playing a trick on him. He had removed the stone, properly photographed it, and written copious notes in a journal about where he had found it and the circumstances surrounding the find. He had examined it closely, holding it up to the dim light inside the temple at least that was what everyone was calling it, to see if he could distinguish any markings.

The stone was small, about the size of a half dollar, smooth and without any flaws of any kind. It was a stone that had no business being where it was at. At first he had identified it as simple granite, probably placed there by someone who had gone exploring and stumbled across the temple. Further testing showed no signs of a substance that could have been considered rock of any kind.

As he held it in his hand, his index finger rubbed the smooth surface. He felt a slight sting in his finger and jerked back, as if he had bitten by something. Examining his finger, he saw a small dot of bright red blood. Instinctively he put his finger into his mouth and sucked on the wound. Looking at the finger again he was satisfied that the wound did not amount to anything more serious than a pinprick. He began to wonder what could have caused the sting and came to the conclusion that some mosquito had landed on the stone just as he was touching it. He thought no more of the incident.

Professor Barry Hale had placed the stone in a small box, marked it accordingly, and forgot all about it.

That is until the day he saw it on his desk.

It was shortly after being appointed as head of the archeology department of the college. His classes were not terribly exciting as he had told his students that most archeology was done in the library, pouring over books and old manuscripts that would only give sketchy information at best. When on a dig, it was crucial to be careful not to destroy some rare artifact by digging haphazardly with large shovels.

It had been the last class of the day and he managed to get back to his office to go over the following weeks schedule when he noticed the small stone. It had been sitting on his desk just left of his lamp. He picked it up, examined it carefully, turning it over in his palm. He was sure that it was the same stone from the dig in the Amazon, but had dismissed that idea when he remembered that all of the items had gone to a museum somewhere in upstate New York. He personally had seen to it that everything was shipped properly. He had been very meticulous in the details.

So why was the stone here at this small college in Georgia, sitting on his desk now?

He thought nothing more of it for a few days.

Until the changes had begun.

He had noticed that he had a loss of appetite, that nothing he tried to eat tasted very good. He had not been able to get any sleep and the toll that it was taking on his body was beginning to show. He had consulted his doctor who gave him a prescription, told him that it was probably a bad cold and sent him on his way with instructions to drink plenty of fluids and get as much rest as he could.

It was the next night that he had had the first dream, or at least he thought it was a dream.

He found himself walking on the campus, a full moon above his head and an eerie fog hanging close to the ground. As he walked, he noticed a young girl who seemed to be beckoning to him. He tried to increase the speed of his gait but found that no matter how hard he tried, he could not seem to get any closer to the girl.

As he looked at her, her beckoning smile turned to awe struck terror. Her body lurched forward and stiffened. Her head was then thrown back, revealing the soft flesh of her neck. The professor watched as a small thin red line began to appear just under her chin. It traveled down her chest and ended at her navel, cutting through the fabric of the yellow dress that she had been wearing. The line began to get more and more defined, seemingly growing deeper and wider into the flesh.

Without warning, the girl let out a scream as the entire front of her body opened, like a door opening into another room. Blood poured onto the ground followed by lungs, kidneys, intestines and finally her heart, beating rapidly even after it hit the ground.

The professor woke at this point, bathed in sweat. After a few moments he was able to convince himself that it had been a rather nasty nightmare, probably brought on by the prescription pills that the doctor had ordered for him.

He had been fine walking toward his office the next morning. The sun was bright and the cool breeze kept the temperature mild. He smiled pleasantly at faculty and students alike, not really noticing the haunted looks that they were giving him.

By the time that he had arrived at his office, he had heard the news of the brutal murder that had taken place only the night before. The body of a young coed had been discovered by security in the early hours of the morning hanging in one of the trees near the archeology building. Very few details about the condition of the body were being released but there had been plenty of rumors floating about that the professor could piece together the truth from the absurd.

Sitting in his office, the dream kept returning to his mind in all of its bloody glory. He tried to pour himself into papers that needed to be graded and schedules that should have been updated weeks ago. No matter what he tried, he could not get the look of terror from the young girls face from his dream out of his mind. He thought that he could actually still hear the beating of the heart as it lay below the dangling corpse.

Teaching each of the classes had become an effort in futility and even the students noticed how much of an effort he was putting into the class. There wasn't anything that seemed to interest him and therefore he could not interest the students. By the time lunch had finally come, he decided to cancel the afternoon schedule.

He was sitting in his office trying to get a sandwich to go down when he thought that he had gone to sleep again.

The dream was even more violent than the one the night before. This time he found himself in the boy's locker room at the other side of the campus. A tall student who was there on a basketball scholarship was getting dressed when he looked up and saw the professor. He smiled and asked the professor if there was anything that he could do for him.

The professor only licked his lips and thought of how the soft flesh of this human would taste; how warm the blood would be as it traveled down his throat. How stupid this human was for not running away or even trying to put up a fight.

Professor Barry Hale thought that this dream seemed more real than anything else as he watched himself take out a long knife, one that he recognized from the collection that was safely locked away in a display case just outside his classroom and plunge it into the chest of the boy. He saw the satanic grin on his own face as he carved open the dead body and began to remove organs, sniffing at them, taking in the warm steam rising from the open body. He watched as he began to bite into the sinewy flesh of the heart as it still beat in his blood soaked hands.

Barry woke up with a start, still sitting in his chair safe inside of his office. His forehead was glistening with sweat and he was visibly shaking. He walked on unsteady legs to his bathroom and splashed cold water onto his face. As he looked into the mirror, he noticed the subtle changes in his features. The dark circles under his eyes had become more defined. A small vein in his forehead had begun to stick out more than usual. His hair, once completely black was showing signs of white.

Grabbing his coat, he practically ran out of his office. He never noticed the sandwich that was lying on the carpet next to his desk that he had dropped with the singe bite taken out of it. Small specks of blood had splattered onto the rest of the white bread.

Barry had managed to make it back to his home. Collapsing onto the sofa, he noticed the small lump in his pocket. Reaching in, he pulled out the small stone. It seemed to be glowing and pulsating within his hand.

A wave of hunger coursed through him and he fell once again into a deep sleep.

This time in his nightmare, he was not a mere observer of his own actions. Instead, he was a participant in the killing of the young coed, opening up the body lying on his desk in his office, pulling out the entrails and eating them amid his own maniacal laughter. He bathed in the warm blood, covering himself from head to chest, ripping off his shirt and relishing the feel of the fluid as he rubbed it onto his chest. He reached into the chest cavity of the girl and extracted the heart, smiling as he studied it in the palm of his hand. With a grin he bit into the hard muscle, ripping and tearing it before pulling a piece of it away.

Barry awoke with a scream from his own lips. He checked himself for any signs of blood but could only find the small stone still clutched tightly in his hand.

He decided that he had to make sure.

The campus was dark and foreboding. He made his way to his office, dreading what he would find there.

All of the memories came flooding back to him as he drove along the empty highway, the stone neatly wrapped in a blood soaked towel and now laying on the passenger seat beside him. He wasn't sure where he was going; he only knew that somehow he had to get rid of the cursed stone. Afterwards, he would turn himself in as the campus killer and try to explain the events away. With any luck, they would only lock him away in some mental ward of a state run hospital. At the very least he would get some peace.

The low but very distinct humming sound had begun as soon as the thought of turning himself over to the authorities had entered his mind. He glanced at the towel in the seat and realized that it no longer covered the stone but was lying in the floorboard. He gazed at the stone now pulsating with a brilliant red glow. He heard the pounding as if the thing had a heart beating at a furious pace. He could not take his eyes off the cursed thing as the red glow grew in intensity.

The blare of the horn of the oncoming tractor trailer made

him jump as he swerved to avoid the collision. Over correcting, he swerved back into the oncoming lane. The tires made a horrible screeching sound as the car plummeted through the safety rail and down the seventy foot embankment.

Barry thought in the last moments of his life that he heard the stone laughing as it was thrown clear of the car. For a brief moment, his mind thought that the stone had jumped clear, leaving Barry to face the large tree ahead of him alone.

As the car hit the tree, it exploded in a brilliant flame.

Barry Hale, professor of archeology was now only a statistic of the highway patrol on that night.

The stone lay a few hundred yards from the wreckage, and waited.

****

CHAPTER ONE
April 27th, 2010

John Tanner looked at the house that had been built on the side of a mountain. The view was fantastic and he could not wait to see what it would look like on the balcony in the rear of the house. The structure was sound and showed no signs of age, even though it was at least ten years old if not older. He loved the wraparound porch with its wooden lattice work. There were only two steps from the driveway to the porch and the front door.

His wife, April and their eight year old son, Bobby were busy walking around the front grounds and stretching their legs from the two and a half hour drive from Atlanta. He smiled as he watched his wife go through her yoga exercises to loosen the muscles in her legs and back. His son was trying his best to mimic his mother, stretching his arms and waving them around.

My family, he thought to himself.

"Hey dad," Bobby yelled out, "do you think that we could get a dog now?"

John smiled at his son and said, "Let's just see if we can get the house first and then we will talk about a dog."

"Hot dang!" Bobby yelled out, using his favorite curse word which his parents allowed him every once in a while.

"How much of this do you think would be ours?" April asked as she walked up to him. The intoxicating smell of her perfume drifted on the air as her long blond hair softly wafted in the breeze of the mountain.

"That I don't know," John admitted admiring his wife's curvaceous form. She was wearing a printed blouse that ended just below her slim waist. The black tights that she had opted for accented her long legs and John began to have fantasies of making love under a full moon on the deck of their new home. He had considered himself one of the lucky few that had found not only a beautiful woman for his wife, but also one that loved him just as much. "I guess we can find that out when the real estate agent gets here."

"I already love this place," she said as she looked around, "it feels like home."

"Now don't go and get your hopes up too much," John warned her. "In the first place, we haven't even seen the inside and at such a ridiculously low price I wonder what could be wrong with it."

"Give me a for instance," she said.

"There could be a horrible termite problem," he answered. "There could be thousands of dollars worth of plumbing or electrical work that needs to be done or the flooring might be rotted. With a house like this you never know."

She smiled up at his six foot two frame and said, "I think that we are going to be pleasantly surprised. When is that agent supposed to be here?"

"He should have met us already," John admitted. He looked at his watch that had been a father's day present just after Bobby was born. His first present since the birth of his only child and he had treasured it for the past eight years. "Maybe he had some car trouble."

"I hope he gets here soon," she said, "I'm dying to see the inside. I hope that there is at least a study or an extra bedroom for my junk."

"Honey, seven successful novels doesn't make anything that you have junk," he told her. "Besides, if you had not been a successful author I would not have been able to take this little sabbatical."

"Is that what you are calling it?" she asked with a smirk. "I thought that you had told Randolph Dickhead to take his job and shove it up his ass."

"His name is Peters and yes, I did hand in a resignation," he said. "What I told him was that if my twelve PhD's with two

Master's in Science wasn't enough for his liking then he could find someone else to do his work. Apparently it worked wonders deflating his ego."

The smile on John's face gave away the news that he had been keeping from April.

"He wants you back," she said flatly.

"At a forty percent increase in pay," he told her with a grin.

"My love," she began slowly, "you know I want you to be happy in anything that you want to do. I will support and love you for eternity, but if you go back to work for that dickhead, I swear you had better hope that we have a very comfortable sofa for you to sleep on."

John laughed and said, "Do you honestly think that I would accept his offer? Honey, that place was killing me, and not doing a whole lot for our marriage. Leaving that shithole was the best decision I had ever made in my entire life. Besides, with a millionaire for a wife, who the hell needs to work?"

"I am very proud of you, husband," she said and cupped his face in her hands before kissing him deeply.

"Ewww," Bobby said, scrunching his face up. "You two are kissing again!"

"All the time, big guy," John said.

"That's gross," Bobby said and ran back toward the edge of the woods where he had been exploring.

"I hope the schools around here are good," she said, watching her son play.

"I'm sure that they have very fine schools here," John told her although not very sure himself. He had not done the kind of research that he would have normally done before considering such a large purchase. He had no idea what the town below the house was like, what civic organizations were there, what the people were like, and most importantly, what the schools had to offer.

John looked at his watch again and said, "I wonder what's keeping him?"

"Why don't you call him?" April asked.

"No service up here," he told her. "That is one thing that will be on our "must do" list. I hope that they have some kind of cell service available."

"I am sure that they do," April said and kissed her husband again.

Yes, John thought to himself, I am really the luckiest man alive. He pulled her in closer as their tongues met and entwined. He ran his large hand gently down her spine, making her moan. He wanted to take her right there on the front lawn, exploring her body with his hands and tongue before penetrating her.

"Later, babe," she said, pulling away from him. "Believe me, it won't be much later."

April had been correct in her feeling. John was feeling it as well. This was indeed home.

Kendal Martin was late.

As he glanced at the digital clock on the dashboard of his Town and Country, he slammed an open hand against the steering wheel, admonishing himself for not leaving sooner.

He was always late, he thought to himself. Everything about him was late. According to his mother, he had been born late, waiting almost ten months before coming out to the big bad world. He was late in graduating high school by a full year due to an illness that nearly cost him his young life. He was late in taking the final tests for his college graduation. He was late when he married a year later. He was late for the birth of their child and when the child passed away six months into its life, he was late for the funeral. He practically almost missed the court hearing for the divorce and was always late in making payments to his ex-wife for the so called alimony that the judge had awarded her.

He had made many attempts to change but no matter what he tried, he was always late. Car payments, rent, bills that were due, everything about him ran late. It wasn't that the bills did not get paid, he thought, it was that he was spending a small fortune in fee's and penalties.

Even with the largest deal of his real estate career on the line, he was running late. He laughed a little at the reason for his tardiness for the meeting and possible sale of the white whale on Wilson's Bluff.

He had a lunch date with girlfriend number four after the divorce before meeting with the Tanner's. Naturally, something had come up at the office and he had been late for lunch, much to the chagrin of Sandra.

Just the thought of her name made him smile. She was ten years younger than him, much more optimistic and always had a smile on her face. Her curly red hair which grew below her neckline cupped a rounded cherub like face with a small nose and very large eyes. She considered herself well proportioned but in truth, she was about fifty pounds overweight for her five foot six height.

He could not understand why she had even talked to him the first day that they had met in the coffee shop on the square. Here he was, fifty three with a pronounced balding spot on the back of his head, thirty pounds over-weight himself with a protruding belly, and definitely not the contender for male model of the year. Somehow, someway, the gods of love had thrust them together six months ago and now they were seriously discussing the possibility of moving in together.

He thought back on the luncheon while driving to meet the potential buyers.

"I'm late," she had said matter of factly.

He kissed her on the forehead and sat down at the table in the same coffee shop where they had first laid eyes on each other.

Laughing, he said, "Don't you mean that I'm late?"

"No, Kendal," she said seriously, "I don't mean that at all. I'm late with my, well, you know."

Kendal looked at her and the dawning of truth hit him right between the eyes.

"Wait, are you sure?" he asked.

"Well," she began, "I haven't been to the doctor or pissed on a stick, but I do know my body and its functions. I have never been late before, and frankly, I'm a little scared. What do you think?"

Kendal looked at her as if for the first time and realized how much he really loved this woman. He smiled and said, "I think that we are going to make wonderful parents."

She smiled and said, "God, I was hoping that you would say that. Hon, I'm sorry."

"Nothing to be sorry about, babe," he told her. "However, I guess we do need to make some plans. First, you need to see a doctor. After that, we can decide which house we are going to need. Personally, I hope that it's twins, but triplets would be nice too."

"And ruin my girlish figure?" she said which made them both laugh.

It had been a very good luncheon. Now, he was driving like mad up the winding road of Wilson's Bluff to hopefully sell a house, get a commission large enough to add to his savings and then search for his own house that would be conducive to raising a family. The one bedroom apartment that he currently lived in was fine for the time being, but nothing that he wanted to dwell in for the rest of his life. His dream had always been to own a modest house where he could be comfortable.

As he pulled into the driveway, he saw the couple standing on the lawn. A young boy was digging around the ground at the edge of the woods. He smiled and thought that this would be the perfect family that he himself would someday have, perhaps sooner than he thought. His mind transferred him to a similar family standing on the front lawn, two, perhaps three children playing and his own arm entwined around his wife's waist. He very much liked the vision and instantly liked the people he saw standing on the front lawn, patiently waiting for his arrival.

Grabbing the keys from his briefcase, he got out of his car with a large smile and called out, "You must be the Tanner's."

John Tanner was a tall and very handsome man. He extended his hand in greeting and said, "You must be the real estate agent."

"Kendal," he told them, shaking the mighty hand vigorously. "Kendal Martin, and no sir, I am not a mere real estate agent. No, I like to think of myself as more of a dream merchant. I buy and sell homes, that is a fact, but I like to think that when I sell a home to, say, a couple such as you, I am selling not just a place to live, but a dream come true."

Oh this guy was good, John thought. "I'm John Tanner, out of work scientist and this is my heiress wife, April."

Bobby came running up behind Kendal and yelled, "Can we go in now?"

"That little tornado is named Bobby," April said. "Can you at least say hello to Mr. Martin, Bobby?"

"Hello," Bobby said. "Now can we go in?"

The three adults laughed.

Kendal made sure that he had the right keys as Bobby ran up to the porch. The others followed slowly behind.

"You know," Kendal began, "I can't shake the feeling that I know that name, April Tanner, from somewhere but I cannot place it. You aren't an actress are you?"

"No," April said, "I am much worse than that. I write horror and mystery fiction."

Kendal stopped on the porch and turned toward her.

"You aren't that April Tanner," he began. "House Of Darkness, Evil Street, Love Child, that author?"

"Guilty as charged," she told him with a winning smile.

"My girlfriend is going to flip when I tell her," he said. "I personally don't like the horror genre, no offense, but my girl, Sandra Sanford, has read everything that you have published. She is just going to flip."

"Tell her that I really appreciate it," April said. "I tell you what; let me give you a copy of my latest book. I'll even sign it for you."

"Oh that would be wonderful," Kendal exclaimed. "She is really going to flip out."

After that, Kendal found it very difficult to open the door.

He smiled and turned back to the young couple and said, "Sometimes these doors stick a little when they haven't been opened in a long time."

With that, the door unlocked and creaked opened.

Nervously, Kendal said, "A little oil will fix that. Well, welcome to your new home," he said, allowing the family to enter first before following them. Even though he had not been inside the house since he acquired the listing, he was able to fake his way through a tour. Showing off some of the more welcoming attributes of the home, especially the four bedrooms and the two full bathrooms, he managed to try and sell the home that for over ten years had remained empty.

Kendal whispered a silent prayer that this nice couple would indeed be the new owners of the home before saying, "Well, except for the basement that is about it. If you folks want to go down and see it you will find the door just down the hallway. Personally, and I hope you folks won't hold this against me; I have a dreaded fear of basements. Don't know where it comes from. I guess I'm a little claustrophobic when it comes to dark places. If you folks need anything, I will be right outside."

"Pleasant enough fellow," John remarked as they made their way to the basement.

"I suppose," April allowed. "I guess 'you folks' ought to at least see the whole house."

John snickered.

The basement ran the full length of the house. Except for the supporting beams the couple agreed that it would be perfect for almost anything and practically everything. April picked out a spot for the laundry area. John picked out a corner for what little work he may have. April said that she could even create an office but was leaning more toward one of the bedrooms that had a view of the valley and the small town that lay directly below them. Billy decided that the entire basement would soon be his spaceship, complete with captain's quarters and galley.

"So my love," John said as Bobby raced back up the stairs and out to the woods again, "do we purchase this place or keep looking?"

She kissed him again, long and deep, giving him the answer to that silly question.

Kendal was standing by his car waiting for some sort of decision. Most of the time a young couple would want to look at a few more listings before deciding on anything. There would then be the financial side of the buying and eventually when all papers were signed and sealed, the deal would close. He watched as the young boy played just inside the tree line of the woods that surrounded the property.

To be young again, he thought to himself.

"Mr. Martin?" John called out as he stepped out of the house with his wife.

"So, you folks like what you see?" Kendal asked nervously.

"Very much so," April answered.

"Fantastic," Kendal said.

"I do have a few questions," John began. "How much of this property would be ours?"

"There is a total of 4.97 acres listed on the deed including the house. According to the county ordinance, you are allowed to clear and use about an acre. The rest of it has to remain untouched. Something to do with not letting in developers who would use every square inch they could get their hands on," Kendal informed them.

"So, the woods around us will basically be ours?" April asked.

"Yes ma'am," Kendal answered. "Oh, you can post no hunting signs around but as to cutting down and developing something, that is strictly forbidden."

"Now for my biggest question," John began.

Kendal held his breath.

"Why such a small amount of money for this place?" John asked. "I would think that you could probably get five times the amount that you are asking."

That was the question, the one thing that Kendal had been dreading since making his way up the winding road. He thought for a moment, perhaps seeing if he could come up with some extravagant lie that they might find plausible.

He decided to stick with the truth.

"Look, "he began, "you folks seem like really nice people, so I'm going to level with you. I really don't know why the place has stayed empty for so long. I was given the listing ten years ago when the last family had the house."

"What happened?" April asked. "Is there a curse on the place?

Did someone die here and now their ghost haunts the place?"

"Spoken like a true horror writer," John said which got him a slight punch on the arm.

"No, nothing like that," Kendal said. "As far as I know, there have only been two occupants since the place was built a little over ten years ago. Thaddeus Kendrick owned all of this property and decided to let his son run the business and do some developing. This was the first house that they built.

"It's a little funny but, now that I think about it, there was a death associated with the house while it was being constructed."

"Really?" John asked.

"Well, you know how these stories start," Kendal said trying desperately not to make it sound as bad as it sounded. "It seemed they were always running into problems up here. Freak storms would pop up out of clear blue skies, tools would come up missing, and orders for supplies were always running late. For a while, Chad Kendrick thought about shutting down the whole project. That is the son of Thaddeus and he actually owns the construction company now that his father has passed.

"Anyway, there was this one worker, can't recall the name, but he kept saying that he saw something in the woods, like a small red glowing light. Everyone must have thought that he was just seeing some sort of reflection or it was just his imagination. Well, he kept looking for whatever was causing the light. One day, he came to work, stood around staring at the woods for about an hour. Then he got in his truck, drove home, put a shotgun in his mouth and blew his head off."

"How awful," April exclaimed.

"No one knew what happened," Kendal continued. "He didn't leave a note or anything, just up and killed himself. After that, construction continued and there were never any more problems. The house was built and sold after about two weeks. As for anyone dying or being killed inside the house, not to my recollection, but then, as I told you Mrs. Tanner, I really don't go into the horror or detective story, fact or fiction."

"It almost sounds like the beginning of a pretty good horror novel," she said as she glanced toward her son, playing happily by the woods.

Bobby watched his parents talking to the real estate agent as he sat just at the edge of the woods. He was quite involved in a game that involved several sticks and stones and bits of earth and the leaves. He was constructing something that resembled a small house, taking away bits of twigs or leaves only to replace them again with something else.

He looked away from his project to see the adults having what appeared to be a very earnest discussion, pointing around at the wooded area and then looking back at the house. Hopefully, he thought to himself, this would be his new home. Upon first seeing the lot as his father drove up, he could sense immediately something very special. He felt that he belonged to the place. Not just the house itself although that would have been grand, but he felt that the woods were calling to him somewhere deep inside his mind. He couldn't quite place the exact feeling that he was having, only that it was there inside him.

He watched a small bug crawl from under a leaf and make its way toward the tiny house like structure. He wondered what the bug must be thinking, that perhaps God had provided some sort of shelter for those cold winter nights. The bug stopped momentarily at the makeshift entrance before crawling in its buglike way inside.

Bobby smiled and began to find small stones and pebbles to make a sort of driveway leading up to his project. He was very meticulous in placing each stone in its proper place, creating a rather unique looking path for whatever bug might happen upon the occupant. He thought that even bugs would probably want to entertain their friends.

He looked up again at his parents and the agent. He saw his mother give him a glance and he waved to her, making sure that she knew that he was fine. No, he would not go wandering around the woods, just as he had promised his mother that he wouldn't do while they were there. Although, he thought, it might be quite an adventure. Perhaps the woods carried some secret cave where some bank robber from long ago had hidden his loot and was killed before he could retrieve it.

He was busy with this line of fantasy when he saw the small stone, just out of reach of where he was sitting. It was the perfect stone for him to finish the driveway to his small twig constructed house and would be a nice centerpiece for the bug and all of his bug friends. They would comment on how nice the stone looked, sitting right there in the middle of the driveway.

Bobby's thoughts were driven away by the sudden bright flash that seemed to come from the stone. He watched harder to see if it had might have been some sort of weird reflection from the sun. He got to his feet and brushed off the remnants of dirt left on his knees and made his way deeper into the woods, keeping his eye on the stone that was so perfect.

"Damn," Bobby muttered as he realized that he had knocked over the bug's house with one step. No matter, he could always build another one. Right now, the most important thing in the whole wide world was the stone that at first had only been within an arm and a half reach from where Bobby sat.

"That's funny," Bobby said aloud as he watched the place where he was sure he had seen the stone. Now it had completely vanished from his sight. It was funny to him because his dad had often commented about how you could see something while sitting down and know exactly what you are looking at, only to discover that it was not the same thing that you thought it was when you stood up. He used a rather big word, something that had to do with how one looks at things. His dad was always using big words.

Bobby took a couple of steps, standing by a very tall oak tree that was like a sentinel, standing guard at the edge of the enchanted forest. He waited for a moment, thinking that the tree would grab him and shake him, demanding what he was doing in the sacred forest of the Tree God.

There! He was sure that he saw the stone flash again, a brilliant red color like that of a ruby. The flash was something like the flash of a camera's flash bulb going off, but this time, Bobby was sure that he knew exactly where the stone was. He took a few more steps into the woods, looking back to make sure that he could still see his parents standing in the yard and discussing details about the house and the grounds. With slow and deliberate footsteps, he inched his way toward the mysterious object.

"That's it?" he said aloud.

He saw the small stone looking like any other stone. There was no longer anything special about it, no brilliant flash of red light, and no mystery at all. He found himself disappointed by the whole thing.

Shrugging his small shoulders, he bent down to pick up the stone for his collection of other artifacts that he had discovered. He had decided that it would be placed in the wooden box that he had made in school three years ago.

"Ouch!"

He pulled his hand back and saw the small red dot on his fingertip. Instinctively, he began to suck his index finger making the blood flow stop. Inspecting his finger and satisfied that there was no major artery broken, he bent down to pick up the stone again.

This time, he looked closer at it, turning it over in his small hands, caressing the smooth surface. It was no larger than a quarter and mostly unremarkable. For a moment he thought about tossing it further into the woods, perhaps to be found a million years later by another small boy.

Something told him not to do that, to take the stone and put it in his pocket.

He was just about to do just that when he looked around for the first time since finding the stone. He could only see the woods, surrounding him and seeming to close in on him. His heart began to beat faster as he realized that perhaps he had wandered a little too far into the tree line. He could not see the house or his parents. He could not see the driveway that held the sanctuary of the car away from the woods. The only things that he could see were the trees now appearing ominous. The limbs looked as if they were reaching for him like the arms of a skeleton, trying to grab at him and rip away his clothes before tearing into his flesh.

His breathing became more labored as his heart pounded away, threatening to tear itself from his chest.

He screamed.

"I think that you will find living around here very pleasant," Kendall said as Bobby screamed.

The three adults turned and saw Bobby at the edge of the woods. April ran towards him in a panic, her thoughts jumping to worse case scenarios. Was it a snake? A bear? A prehistoric creature? Something had made her little boy scream and she would face the hounds of hell to defeat it and make it pay.

"Bobby? What happened?" April said breathlessly as she reached for her son. Her hands began to check every part of him for signs of blood or broken bones.

"Is he ok?" John asked as him and Kendal approached.

"I cut my finger," Bobby lied, although the blood had started again.

April inspected the finger and saw the small droplet. She smiled at her son and reassured him that he was in no danger.

"Probably a briar," Kendal offered. "The woods are full of them. That's why you got to be careful, son."

"Mr. Martin is right," John told his son. "Are you going to be ok, big guy?"

"Sure dad," Bobby said, feeling a whole lot better now that the forest had retreated back to its original state. "Hey, dad, look what I found."

"In a little bit," John told him, "let me finish up some business with Mr. Martin and then we can go into town and get a celebration meal."

"We are getting the house?" April asked, standing next to the two men with Bobby firmly in her grip.

Kendal Martin's heart did a somersault as he had hoped that the words were actually being said by this nice young couple.

"If he can produce the contracts," John began, "I do believe that this man has just sold himself a house."

"I have them in my car," Kendal exclaimed and almost tripped running back to get the paperwork. He thought about the nice commission that would come out of the sale and how he would be able to afford leaving the town and opening somewhere else. Dreams of an extravagant wedding were dancing in his brain as he fumbled with the car door desperately trying to open it.

John Tanner looked at his wife and son, both wearing smiles. He loved them both very dearly and wanted to give them everything that he could. A new house away from the hustle of the city was only the beginning. As he signed the contracts for Kendal, he felt glowing pride that his family would have very little to worry about.

****

CHAPTER TWO

"Buying a house is a whole lot easier than moving into one."

John was carrying the box of kitchen utensils from the moving van and was already starting to feel the pain in his back. As he put the box onto the floor, he stretched and heard the tissue creak and groan.

April smiled and kissed him as she bent down to open the box and pulled out the most essential items for her first dinner in her brand new home.

"Pizza is sounding better and better," John told her.

"I don't think so mister," she admonished him. "We have been living in a motel for two weeks waiting for money to clear and permits and whatever else someone can think of to keep us from moving in. Tonight, I am cooking for my two men."

"What are cooking, mom," Bobby said as he came storming into the kitchen.

"Hey, where did you come from?" John asked as he scooped his son up into his arms.

"Putting my animals up so that they can protect us," Bobby told him.

"Do you like your room?" April asked as she began to busy herself with the preparation for cooking their first meal.

"It's ok," Bobby said.

"Just ok?" John asked and looked at his son. He felt nothing but love for the small child that had come from the womb of the woman that he had pledged his life to. He looked into the young eyes, noticing the flecks of brown that were embedded into the hazel color. He felt that he knew instinctively every hair on the child's head.

"Yes, dad," Bobby answered, "I like it very very much. Satisfied?"

For only a split second, John thought that he saw something else in his son's eyes, something that didn't belong. It was the way that Bobby had answered him that took him aback.

"What kind of tone is that, mister?" April asked as she stopped abruptly and turned to them.

"Can I go now?" Bobby said and squirmed in his father's arms.

Letting the boy down gently, John said, "Go on, but don't go too far away from the house. Your mom will have dinner ready soon."

Bobby only waved his hand and left his parents standing in the kitchen, watching him as he made his way back to his room.

"That was odd," April commented as she continued to put utensils away.

"Probably just the jitters of moving into a new home," John said.

April put the last spoon into its proper place and turned to her husband with a smile.

"Hello, sexy," John said with a salacious grin. She was wearing a t-shirt and some old jeans that still contoured to her legs, but to him, she was a definite super model.

She began to walk towards him in a cat like manner, her arms swaying from side to side as she bounced each hip to a sexy rhythm. Her lips parted as she ran her tongue across her teeth, flicking it out slightly and wiggling it like a snake.

"Keep this up and we may have to break in the house right here," John told her. Taking her into his arms, their mouths met in a torrent of passion. He could feel April's body gyrating against him as her tongue slid into his mouth meeting his own.

Breaking away, April stepped back and said, "Consider this a preview of coming attractions, handsome. Now go and finish getting the boxes for the kitchen."

"Slave driver," he joked as he headed back to the rented truck.

The furniture had arrived the day before and now the only things left were the few personal belongings that the family had managed to pack in a short amount of time. April had been in charge of telling the men where each piece would go and John and Bobby were assigned the dubious task of unloading various articles that would go into the garage. Tonight, with the truck unloaded, they would spend their first night in their new home. Each one of them was excited with the anticipation of actually sleeping without the noises from the city.

Bobby sat on the front lawn, watching his father carry yet another box into the house. He wasn't sure why he had talked to his dad in the manner which he had, it had just come out of nowhere. He normally would have never said something like that to either one of his parents. He loved them both.

There was that split second, somewhere deep inside of him, that welled up and came spewing out. It was almost a deep seated hatred for the people who were standing in the kitchen. Bobby could not explain where it had come from, but he found that he actually enjoyed the momentary feeling of defiance that he had shown to his parents.

The stone sat in his hand motionless. Bobby squeezed it, caressed it, twirled it between his fingers, but mostly he only stared at it. For the past two weeks of living in a motel room, he had found himself taking the stone from his special box more and more. He would hold it in his hands for hours looking deeper and deeper into it. The strange light that he thought that he had first seen had never appeared yet something was willing him to simply hold the stone.

"Hey, big guy," John said making Bobby jump. "What do you have there?"

"Just a rock," Bobby answered.

"Really? Let's see," John said and reached for it.

"No, it's mine!" Bobby yelled and pulled away from his father.

"Hey, easy there," John said and knelt down beside his son. "I just wanted to have a quick look."

Bobby slowly opened his hand so that his father could see the stone.

"Looks pretty neat," John told him. He wanted to get a closer look at it but was afraid of another outburst from his son. This was supposed to be a special day and John did not want something so trivial as a rock to interfere with it.

"Where did you find it?" John asked.

Bobby pointed to the edge of the woods and said, "The day we came up to look at the house I thought I saw something in the woods. It turned out to be just an old rock. I tried to show it to you that day but you were busy, as always."

That little remark cut John a little but he decided to let it go.

"Maybe," John said, trying to placate his son and salvage the day, "it's a protection stone."

Bobby looked up at his father for the first time that day with wonder.

"What's a protection stone?" he asked.

John smiled and said, "Well, from what I have heard and some of the history that I have studied, a protection stone is usually the first rock that the new owners find on the property that they have just acquired. They take the stone into the house and place it in a prominent place. It is said that as long as the stone remains there, the house and all who dwell in it will be protected from any evil."

"Really, dad?" Bobby said thinking that maybe his father was making something up.

John held up his hand and said, "Scout's honor."

"So, should we put this one up somewhere so we are protected?" Bobby asked, his index finger caressing the smooth stone.

"Unless you have a better use for it," John said. "We could maybe put it on the mantel above the fireplace in the front room. It can sort of watch the windows and doors from that point and according to the legend; no evil will be able to enter the house."

Bobby thought for a minute and said, "Ok."

John smiled and asked to see the stone a little closer. Bobby handed it to him and ran back into the house.

He looked after his son and then examined the stone. Just like the vision that he had briefly seen in his son's eyes while in the kitchen, he could have sworn that he saw a faint glow coming from the stone. Shaking his head, he looked again and only saw the small rock in his hand.

"Damn!" he exclaimed, dropping the stone into the grass.

Looking at his hand he saw the tiny droplet of blood in his palm.

"Must have been an ant," he thought to himself.

****

CHAPTER THREE

The sun was beginning to set and the slight wind made the trees around the house sway. The mountain air was clean and fresh. The first stars of the night were beginning to dot the twilight sky. Birds that had been active the entire day were nestling down making way for the chorus of crickets, giving a new symphony to the forest.

April and John Tanner sat on the porch of their new home, holding hands and watching as the sky began to turn from a bright orange to a soft blue. Their first home cooked meal of steak and baked potato with a green salad to compliment had long since been digested and the couple was enjoying the prospect of living out their lives in their new home. Bobby was lying on the front lawn, looking up at the ever darkening sky. He had always liked to look at the far away stars, their light from millions and perhaps billions of years ago just now reaching the atmosphere of the Earth had always fascinated him.

"Beautiful night," April said.

John looked at his wife and smiled.

"Dinner was fantastic," John said to her. "I still don't think that I can move."

April laughed. "Don't get too use to the idea of meals like that, mister. After tonight it just might be pizza and tacos from town."

"Suits me," John said. "I can't have my wife getting bad habits like slaving in the kitchen when she should be slaving in front of a typewriter."

"You mean the computer," she corrected, "and I am not exactly slaving."

"I thought you said you were having some problems with the

latest horror show?" he asked her.

"That's the strange thing," she answered. "I really was until sometime this afternoon while I was cooking. You were outside with Bobby and had just come back in. It was like a lightning bolt that hit all at once. I knew exactly where I wanted the story to go and how to get there. I stopped cooking long enough to get the general idea on paper before I forgot it."

"Is it going to be a good story?"

"Oh, I think so," April said with a sly grin.

"Do I get a chance to read this latest masterpiece?"

"Not until I have put the final touches on it," she told him, "now you know that."

"Yes, I do," he agreed and settled back on his elbows.

The sun had all but disappeared and the night air was getting crisper against their skins. April stood up and called for her son who reluctantly got off the ground and sauntered inside the house. John, his muscles still aching from the heavy lifting made his way slowly into the house with his family.

"I guess we still don't have TV," Bobby commented.

"They said that they would hook the cable up tomorrow," April told him. "The internet is included along with the telephone so you will just have to do something else tonight. Why don't you try drawing something? You haven't done that since we moved up here."

"I suppose," Bobby said and slowly made his way up to his room.

April cast a worried glance to John.

"Does he seem all right to you?" she asked as Bobby disappeared down the hall toward his bedroom.

"Fine to me," John said and settled into the easy chair. All of the furniture had been arranged to April's watchful eye and the easy chair, that old tattered thing as she had called it, had almost been thrown out. John begged her to let it stay and she acquiesced against her better judgment. It was the first chair that they had bought together after they had married and John did not have the heart to throw it away. He could point out every stain and tear that had been made on it and tell you exactly when it had happened and what the circumstances were at the time. To John, the chair was more than just a comfortable piece of furniture, it was a memory book.

"You in that god awful chair," April said as she sat on the nice new sofa across from him.

"Don't knock the chair," John warned playfully. "Besides, it isn't the chair you want to talk about it."

"You're right, it isn't," she agreed. "Haven't you noticed the way Bobby has been acting?"

"I told you," he said, "he's just a little nervous about the new house, the new school, new friends, basically new everything."

"Honey, we have moved before and he didn't act this way," she said.

"That is because he was two years old when we moved from one apartment to another one," he reminded her. "This is quite a step and he is a bit older now. The only thing that I have noticed is a typical ten year old boy who has been thrust headfirst into a new situation and this is how he is handling it."

"Spoken like a true scientist," she said with a smile.

"He is going to be fine," he said, as if that were to be the final word on the matter.

"Still, I'm a little worried," April continued. "I don't think that he likes school very much."

"What kid at that age does?" John asked. "Look, it is right at the end of the school year and the school here doesn't go by the same curriculum that his old school did, so naturally he is going to feel a little lost. He already had the grades to move on, didn't he? This was just to keep the powers that be off of us until summer vacation which is in about three weeks. Believe me, honey, he will be fine."

"I guess you're right," April said.

"Oh, I almost forgot," John said and practically leaped out of the chair.

Heading toward the kitchen he went directly to the fridge. Opening the door he reached in toward the back and pulled the bottle of Chianti that he had hoped he had hidden well enough from his wife. Rummaging through an open box he managed to find two wine glasses from their collection that he hoped to have hanging up by tomorrow. He found the corkscrew in the box of utensils that still sat on the floor. Quickly he made his way back to the living room and sat on the sofa beside his wife, producing the bottle and glasses from behind his back.

"Oh, John," she said with a little disappointment.

"Well, what's the matter?" he asked.

"You have been on the wagon for almost seven years, honey," she reminded him. A glint of understanding showed in her eyes when she said, "That was why you went back into town. All that jazz about the wrong brand of salad dressing was just your way of going and getting this."

"Honey, it's okay," he assured her. "One small glass of wine is not going to send me down the road to hell. Besides, isn't this what you're supposed to do when you move into a new home?"

"You had better explain that to me or else I have missed something," she said.

Smiling, he said, "We have broken bread, we must use salt to keep away anything evil, and we must consecrate the house with a toast, using very good Chianti."

"Where, pray tell, did you come up with that line of crap?"

"It's a Wonderful Life," he said, "Jimmy Stewart and Donna Reed, 1947."

"Well," she said with a dubious grin, "at least it is a good brand."

Taking the bottle from her, he inspected the label and remarked, "Apparently a good week too," which brought them both to fits of laughter.

As he extracted the cork with a little effort, the aroma of the wine filled the air. Pouring the glasses full, he raised his and said, "May this be the last house that we ever live in, to be handed down to our great great grandchildren." Clinking the glasses together, they drank.

As the wine filled his mouth, John glanced toward the mantel above the fireplace. He noticed the small stone again which seemed to be radiating from a brilliant light deep within the rock. It only happened for a split second but was enough to make him choke a little on the wine. April patted his back amidst the fit of coughing.

"I'm ok," John said, sputtering a little. "It has been seven years, hasn't it?"

Taking his glass and sitting it on the floor beside the sofa, she stroked his cheek before kissing him long and deep.

"Do you think Bobby is asleep yet?" he asked.

"Why don't you go upstairs and see," she whispered, "and then meet me back here."

"On the sofa?" he asked.

"We have to start somewhere, don't we?" she asked with a sly grin.

"Back in ten minutes," he said and stood up.

"Ten minutes?" she asked as she peeled off her shirt. Her satin bra clung to her breasts and she began to stroke the ever hardening nipple with her index finger.

"Make that five," he said and hurried up the stairs.

The sex was long and intense, consecrating not only the sofa but most of the floor of the living room. Both were covered in sweat as they lay panting on the floor beside the empty fireplace. Their hands intertwined and John kissed each of his wife's fingertips, sending another wave of wanting through both of them. Smiling, April began kissing his chest, moving farther down and engulfing him, determined to get one more orgasm from him.

Twenty minutes later, John, breathing heavily said, "Wow."

"I concur," April said as she lay back on his chest, her fingers dancing along his still firm stomach.

"Anymore wine left?" he asked.

"That was gone two hours ago," she told him.

They lay together for the better part of an hour, listening to the sounds of the silent house, the myriad creaks and groans that seem to only occur late in the night. They were totally at one with each other, their bodies and souls connected through the act of unadulterated sex. The only other sounds in the room were the steady breathing that each of them were managing after the love making.

April raised herself up and looked down at the perfect body of her perfect lover. Smiling, she began to caress her own breast, enticing him.

"Are you kidding?" John asked.

"Don't you want me?" she asked with a seductive grin which led to her putting her finger into her mouth and sucking.

"In the worst way," John answered, "but I don't think I'm physically able to, although my oral skills might be useful right about now."

Grabbing her, John forcefully laid his wife down, spread her legs and plunged his tongue inside her bringing her to an instant orgasm. He remained there for a long time, hearing his wife moan, making her rise and fall with waves of passion.

"Jesus," she finally said after he allowed her to rise up again. "It has been a long time since you have done that to me."

"Did you enjoy yourself?" he asked teasingly.

"Very much so," she answered.

Standing up, he found his pants that had been thrown into a corner and pulled them on.

"What are you doing?" she answered, lying back on the floor, feeling the coolness of it against her back.

"I think that I had better check on Bobby," he said. "Do you think that perhaps you could rustle up something to eat? I'm starved."

April finally realized that she was also famished.

"I'll go and see what we have," she said and made her way naked to the kitchen.

John smiled as he headed up the staircase.

The first thing that he noticed was that the light in Bobby's bedroom was still on, shining brightly under the door. He silently opened the door and found Bobby slumped over at his desk, sound asleep.

He marveled at his son for a moment before gently picking him up and putting him into bed. A soft kiss on the forehead confirming his love for the boy and he was ready to return back to his wife and lover.

Just before leaving, he looked over at the desk to see what Bobby had possibly been working on before laying down. His brow furrowed at the picture on the desk that Bobby had done in crayon. His first thought was how hideous the depiction of the house was. All of the lines were crooked and the windows had distinct cracks. Three figures that he assumed were the family was standing outside the house, the stick figures that you might see from any ten year old. They all wore very sad faces except that the figure of Bobby and April had very sharp teeth with bits of red around them.

John looked at some of the other pictures that Bobby had drawn since the age of five hanging up around the room. These were more of his style. There were beautiful landscapes and excellent portraits of not only him and his wife but of other people. These were the pictures of someone who had studied painting for many years but for Bobby it was a talent that he had come by naturally.

He looked down at the grotesque picture again. Quietly, he picked it up and just before leaving the bedroom, he shut the light off and closed the door.

April had managed to find some crackers and cheese in the kitchen. Placing them on a plate, she made her way back to the living room. She was still in the throes of complete fulfillment from the sex, especially the oral gratification that she had received from her husband. Putting the plate on the floor, she stretched onto the sofa, her feet resting on the armrest at the end.

The small flash of red light caught her eye. She rose up, looking around the room for the source of the sudden flicker of light. She was sure that it had come from somewhere around the fireplace. Looking hard she could find no source of light or even a reflection that might have caused the quick flash.

Yet there it was again, just a small almost imperceptible twinkle of red light that she could only see out of the corner of her eye that had now intrigued her. She scanned the fireplace again, standing up and walking over to it, running her hands along the mantle. As she reached toward the top of the mantelpiece, her hand jerked suddenly back as if something had bitten her. Rising up on her toes, she found the small stone that John had placed there earlier in the evening. Picking it up, she held it in her hand carefully. Her finger began to rub the smooth surface and for the first time she realized that something had cut her. The blood on her index finger was smearing into the stone.

She reached up and put the stone back. Returning to her position on the sofa, she sucked the blood from her fingertips, her eyes never leaving the top of the mantel, waiting for the flash of red light to make its appearance again.

After a few moments, she finally admonished herself for thinking that the stone had anything to do with the light. Perhaps it was a passing car shining its lights through the window, she thought to herself. Yes, that was the answer. Who had ever heard of a stone with a flashing light inside?

She picked up a piece of the cheese and began to slowly munch. The aching between her legs had only started up again and she could barely wait for John to get back. Perhaps this was going to be an all night session of passionate sex. It had been a very long time since they had managed to make love until the sun came up, only falling asleep when the bright light bathed them in its warmth.

She noticed another drop of blood on her fingertip and sucked it away. She found herself sucking a little more intently than she realized, almost using her finger as a phallic symbol of oral sex. She moved her finger down her chest, twisting her nipple hard and wincing with the pain. It was as if her hand had developed a mind of its own and was beginning to make love to her. She watched in fascination as her own hand moved toward her clitoris, rubbing and pinching, bringing her to yet another intense orgasm.

Breathing heavily, she was sure that once again, she saw the flash of red light from the mantel.

"What the hell was that?" she said out loud, her breathing heavy. She rose up and sat on the sofa, waiting for John to come back from Bobby's room. In a few minutes, she saw him walk into the room and disrobe before joining her on the sofa.

"Are you ok?" he asked, noticing the new formed sweat on her forehead.

"I'm great," she said, sucking her finger again.

"The food looks great," he told her as he began to eat.

Food was the last thing on her mind now. All she wanted was him inside of her, thrusting hard and filling her, creating more and more waves of passion. She could not hold back any longer as she straddled him, stroking him to full erection before guiding him inside her. She lost all control as she grabbed his hair, her body finding renewed energy as she made him pound into her. At the very height of orgasm, she bent down and bit into his shoulder, drawing a little blood.

"Damn!" he shouted as he felt her teeth dig into his shoulder.

The orgasm for both of them was long and ended with April slumped down on John's chest. John's member was still inside of her, pulsating with its own rhythm. In a few minutes, both of them were fast asleep.

****

CHAPTER FOUR

Around seven in the morning John woke and managed to find his pants before Bobby woke up and found his parents sprawled out on the sofa in all of their naked glory. He imagined the years of therapy it would take for that image to be wiped away. He found one of the moving blankets and covered his wife up just before Bobby walked into the room.

"Is mom all right?" Bobby asked sleepily.

"She's fine, big guy," John told him. "She is just tired from all the events of yesterday. You don't look like you have had much sleep either."

"Oh, I'm ok, I guess," Bobby said as he wiped his eyes.

"Anything going on with school that I need to be aware of?" he asked him.

"Nothing special," Bobby said. "What's for breakfast?"

Breakfast, John thought. Damn good question.

"Tell you what," John began as he pulled on the t-shirt that he had worn the day before, "why don't we go out and grab something in town. Then I can take you to school and you won't have to wait on the bus."

"Sounds good to me," Bobby said, his face lighting up. He had always enjoyed spending time with his father, especially since he knew that his dad could not boil water let alone make breakfast. "Besides, I was hoping for something more than just cereal."

"What is that supposed to mean, young man?" John asked jokingly, although he knew the answer. Cereal was about the only thing that he could do without burning the house down. It amazed him at times that he could cook something up in the laboratory with the ease of a great chef without any problem whatsoever. Try to boil water in the kitchen and there would possibly be a three alarm call arriving at the smoldering remains of the house.

"Is there an IHOP nearby?" Bobby asked.

"Well, let's go and find out," John said.

Bobby ran to the kitchen and picked up his book bag and followed his father out to the car. They had both given April a light kiss on the forehead before departing. John noticed that she never moved, which in itself would have been unusual had he not known what had happened the night before.

"You are welcome," he whispered before leaving.

While the nearest IHOP was about an hour away, they did manage to find a small café that boasted the best biscuits and gravy in the south. Since they both liked the dish, they decided to give it a try. John ordered coffee for himself and milk and orange juice for his son. The waitress was all smiles and cordiality as she took the order.

"Nice place," John muttered.

"I like it," Bobby said.

"Don't take too long in eating," John reminded him, "we still have to get you to school."

"I won't," Bobby answered. "By the way, dad, where did you get that mark on your shoulder?"

"What mark?" John asked as he sipped his coffee.

"That one," Bobby pointed.

"I don't know," John said. "Wait here," he told him and made his way to the bathroom.

Looking in the mirror, he moved his shirt to one side. Indeed, it was not just a mark, but a nasty bruise. He ran his fingers across it and winced at the pain that it caused. He knew full well where it had come from but had not realized that April had bit down so hard on him. He could distinguish the teeth marks among the black and blue bruising. Had she drawn blood?

There had been several times in their marriage, and even before when they had first dated, where the passion had been so great that April had managed to dig her nails into his back leaving scratches. He didn't mind the slight pain or the marks that would appear. He wore them as badges of honor knowing that he had completely satisfied the woman that he had known from the beginning he would share his life with.

This was much more than a simple scratch. She had never bitten him before. He wasn't sure if it was something to be very proud of or perhaps concerned about. He opted not to say anything to his wife about it unless she saw the bruise and asked. He smiled a little at the thought of the conversation that would ensue over a completely satisfying night of fucking.

By the time he got back to the table, Bobby was already half way through the rather large plate of food.

As John sat down, he looked down at his own plate. For a moment, he felt his stomach turn over as the food looked anything like the best in the south. The gravy seemed to be crawling with bugs and insects of all kinds. The biscuits underneath rolled along the plate and then begin to bleed. The dark red fluid began to mix with the whiteness of the gravy making a strange kaleidoscope of sickly colors.

"Dad!"

John looked up at his son, then back at the plate which appeared to be completely normal.

"You ok?" Bobby asked.

The waitress had noticed the concern on the boys face and had made her way back to the table.

"Everything all right, sir?" she asked John.

"Yes," he said looking up into her bright face. "Yes, everything is fine; I guess I had a little too much to drink last night."

Taking the plate of food, she said, "Don't worry about it, I have had mornings like that myself. I'll go and get you a glass of orange juice, always seemed to help me."

She had been right. The juice went down a lot easier than the food would have. He practically swallowed the sixteen ounces in one gulp. The café had not charged him for the uneaten breakfast and by the time Bobby had finished, it was time for another day of school.

Dropping Bobby off at the curb, he noticed one of the teachers waving at him, beckoning him to get out of the car. Thrusting the gear into park, he made his way across the lawn and joined the older lady who indeed looked like the caricature of a teacher from his old high school days. Her face was shining in the sunlight from the mounds of makeup that she wore and her perfume was just a tad overwhelming, the very thing he needed after the incident in the café.

"Mr. Tanner," the teacher said, "I don't think that we have officially met but I am Mrs. Agnes Underhill, your son's art teacher."

"Very pleased to meet you," John said and gently shook the teacher's hand in greeting.

"I was going to send a letter home with your son today," she began, "and ask that you and Mrs. Tanner make time for a conference, but since you are here now, I suppose it was fortuitous of me to be the lucky teacher on bus patrol today."

"Is there something wrong?" John asked with a little concern.

"Oh, I don't think that it is anything to be concerned about," she assured him. "I wonder if you have the time to come inside to my classroom. My first class isn't for another hour and I would like to show you something that I feel is very important for you and your wife to see."

"Of course," John said and followed her into the school house. He glanced and noticed Bobby enter the large building ahead of them, making sure that his son was safely inside.

Down a long corridor of display cases and lockers at the very end of the hall was Mrs. Underhill's room. Lining the walls were pictures that had been done by students that semester. John examined a few and noticed the almost professional mood that came from many of them. The one thing that he did miss was anything that Bobby might have painted or drawn.

Mrs. Underhill sat behind her desk and motioned for John to take a chair on the opposite side. John felt a little ridiculous trying to fit into the small desk seat. He wondered if teachers since the beginning of time had made this their little joke on the parents, showing their superiority over the lowly humans who would dare to think that they and their offspring were better than the mighty teacher.

"The reason that I asked you inside," Mrs. Underhill began, "is that I am a little concerned with your son."

"Has he done something to another student?" John asked.

"Nothing of the kind," she reassured him. "This does not have to do with anything in his behavior. No, your son is a fine young man, very well mannered, always respectful and from what I have seen gets along with practically everyone. No, this has to do with his drawings."

"I don't understand," John said.

Removing a file folder from her desk, she placed it in front of her and opened it up. She turned it around for John to look inside.

Smiling, John said, "I remembered when he painted that one."

The painting was the depiction of a crystal clear lake, the mountains in the background, snow capped and brilliant in their fall colors. In the forefront was the head of a deer, taking a sip from the cool waters of the lake. John had given the picture to the school not as bragging, but to show them the kind of artist that Bobby would someday become. He was years ahead of most other children who had the knowledge to draw and paint.

Mrs. Underhill turned over the picture and showed John the next one.

Again, he smiled as he saw the happy countenance of his own wife, smiling in the charcoal drawn picture. John had managed to talk his wife into letting the school have that one as well to show that Bobby was versatile in almost any style of painting.

Mrs. Underhill turned the page over again and said, "This is one that he drew his first week here. As you can see, it is a remarkable painting of the front of the school. The detail that Bobby has put into this picture shows a much more advanced stage than even I could hope for. He really is quite gifted."

John beamed with pride for his son, until he saw the subtle change in the teachers face to one of concern.

Slowly she turned the picture over to reveal the next painting.

John looked and could almost feel the same nausea from the café returning with a vengeance. It was a horrifying face, one of evil and contempt for anything. Looking closer, he realized that the face was not something that had come from the imagination of a small child, but was more of a self portrait. Take away the anger and hostility from the portrait, and you could very easily see the face of Bobby.

"Do you see what I mean?" Mrs. Underhill asked.

"Yes, I see it, but…"

"Wait," she told him and flipped over to the next one.

More grotesque than the one that John had found on Bobby's desk the night before, this was something that only an insane person who has had a nightmare might draw. It was another depiction of the front of the school, only this time it was distorted and mangled. Streaks of red were drawn all over and John could only assume that this represented blood.

"So I think that you can see why I was concerned," Mrs. Underhill told him. "Are there any problems in the home?"

John looked up from the nightmare drawing and regained his composure, saying, "We just moved into a new house. Other than that, there are no problems."

"I know that your wife is the author of several, well let's just say she is an author," Mrs. Underhill said, treading lightly. "Has Bobby ever read or been allowed to read any of her books or stories?"

"What has that got to do with it?" John asked, a feeling of anger welling up from deep within him.

"Perhaps nothing at all," she said quickly. "I enjoyed Poe and Hawthorne when I was a young girl. I was merely trying to address the fact that the paintings and drawings that your son is attempting to do are showing signs of possible abuse."

And there it was, John thought.

"Are you saying that my wife and I are abusing our son and he is drawing these pictures as a way of acting out?" John asked slowly.

"We have found that when a child suddenly changes, there is

an underlying factor," she back peddled somewhat, but not much.

"Perhaps Bobby is simply going through a phase of exploring different aspects of art," John countered. "Or perhaps you would rather he not have any imagination?"

"I never said that," Mrs. Underhill defended herself. She was beginning to get flustered and wish that perhaps Mrs. Tanner would have been better suited to talk with.

"You know, perhaps home schooling might be better suited for my child," John said.

"Let me assure you, Mr. Tanner, that we have one of the finest schools in the state," she said. "I don't think that it will be necessary to go to that extreme."

"Good day, Mrs. Underwood," John said on purpose. Rising up, he stormed out of the school room.

"That's Underhill," she called after him. Dejectedly, she put the folder of paintings and drawings away, feeling that she probably could have handled the situation a little better.

Bobby stood underneath the window of the room, hidden by the large bushes, listening to the entire conversation. He smiled as a small flicker of red light began showing in his eye.

April was still lying on the sofa, a thin film of sweat covering her naked body. In her dream, she found herself securely tied with silk ribbons to an ornate four poster bed. She began to struggle slightly, feeling the coolness of the fabric against her skin. She could feel the yearning sensation quickly overtake her body. Looking around the bare room, she noticed that there were no windows and no doors. She began to feel apprehensive; telling herself to wake up from what was quickly becoming a nightmare.

She had written several short stories based on her dreams and even her nightmares, but nothing in her past compared with what she was experiencing now. She struggled again with her bonds and felt them cut into her soft flesh. A small trickle of blood began to ooze down her arm. Instead of being disgusted or horrified, she watched in fascination as the blood continued its slow downward journey. Without another thought, she managed to bend her head slightly and lick the blood away from her arm.

"Very good."

Looking at the foot end of the bed, she saw the figure of a well endowed naked man. His face was covered in a black mask with only a small slit for the mouth. She could see his tongue flicking in and out as if he were a cobra getting ready for the kill.

"Who are you?" she asked.

"I am you," the figure answered.

She watched as the male began to change into female. Her apprehensiveness was beginning to grow and now fear had slowly begun to take over. She saw the figure remove the mask and gasped as she saw herself, smiling lasciviously with the same flicking tongue movement.

The female figure approached April and knelt down between her legs, slowly lowering her head toward her sex. She felt the softness of her own tongue begin to lick and caress the inner thigh and for a moment she let the overwhelming sense of erotica take her. She began to writhe slightly, wanting more and more, moaning louder and louder.

Until the exquisite pain that wracked her body penetrated her dream and took her down the road to a full-fledged nightmare. She opened her dream eyes and saw that the figure had changed into something that only Lovecraft could have dreamed up from the bowels of hell. The monster had two horns that curled around its massive head. Another horn extended from its forehead and at the end of it was an exaggerated bloodshot eye. There wasn't any presence of a nose, but the mouth seemed to fill the entire face. Teeth as sharp as any razor filled the cavity and stuck in between them was a mound of flesh, still dripping blood from where it had been bitten off.

April looked down from the thing and saw the blood pouring from the open wound where her sex had once been. Most of her inner thigh had already been chewed away and bone could be visible through the wound.

April awoke with a scream, gasping for air in the stifling confines of the house. Her hair was matted with sweat and her hands were shaking. She managed to get her bearings and quickly scanned the sofa and the sheet that John had provided for any signs of blood. Collapsing back onto the sofa, she began to slowly get her breathing back under control.

A few moments later, she was able to go to the kitchen. Taking a glass she gulped down water from the tap as if she had not had anything to drink in days. Splashing the cool water onto her face, she began to compose herself.

"What the hell was all that about," she muttered to herself.

The ring of the bell brought her fully awake and she realized for the first time that she was completely naked. This didn't exactly bother her. She had spent many days walking around their apartment without clothes on while John and Bobby were away. She would have done the same thing today had the visitor not been so rude as to ring their doorbell.

Running into the living room she called out that she would only be a minute while she found her clothes from the night before. Quickly dressing, she was about to open the door when she realized that she had not found her bra. Her nipples were slightly erect and her breasts were showing through the material.

Oh well, she thought and answered the door.

"Hello," the lady on the front porch greeted her.

"Hello yourself," April replied.

"I'm Nancy Jennings from the closest house to you," the lady said. In her hand was what appeared to be a casserole dish. The aroma coming from it made April realize that she had not eaten breakfast yet.

"I'm April Tanner," she introduced herself. "Won't you come in?"

Nancy smiled and made her way past the lovely young woman with the perky breasts.

"I hope that I am not bothering you," Nancy said.

"No," April replied. "You will just have to forgive the mess. Is that for us?"

Holding the dish out towards April, the lady said, "It is just a simple meal that I thought might come in handy. You can keep the dish, I have dozens of them."

"Thank you, I'll just put this in the kitchen," April said. "At least that takes care of dinner tonight. Make yourself at home."

Nancy pushed the sheet from the sofa and sat down. In the normal fashion of the average person, she began to take stock of the new owners of the home. She noticed the still unopened and half emptied boxes that still remained in the living room. She made no judgment about the mess but thought that she would never had invited someone in if it had been her house. She would have politely taken the dish and then invited them back at a more opportune time when she had finished getting the house arranged for visitors.

April came back a few moments later and said, "I'm sorry about the mess but we did just move in. You must know how hard it is."

"Believe me, you never know what kind of things you actually have until you move them," Nancy agreed. "My late husband and I moved up here and I found a box of my son's toys when he was five years old. I had forgotten that I had even kept them. In a way, it turned out quite all right. It seems that my son was having some financial difficulty at the time. Anyway, he came up for a short visit after we were all settled in and I presented him with the box. What use did I have for it? About two weeks later he informed me that one of the toys, one that he had never actually opened, was worth fifteen thousand dollars! Can you believe it? Like something out of a movie, don't you think?"

April listened to the new neighbor drone on and on. The woman was at least in her mid to late forties, tall, almost statuesque with a sort of hardness about her face. Her hair was long and a fiery red with slight curls at the end. April would not call her dumpy by any means but she could tell that the woman needed to lose at least twenty pounds. What caught her attention the most were the perfectly formed breasts that seemed to be beckoning to her. She could hardly take her eyes off of them.

It was a new experience for April. She had never found herself attracted to another woman, even in college as an experiment in sex, but today was completely different. She felt the yearning sensation from her dream return in a torrential wave across her body.

Looking up, she realized that Nancy Jennings had asked her a question.

"I'm sorry," April said, "I must have been somewhere else."

Nancy smiled showing her perfect white teeth and said, "Honey, I do it all the time. I used to drive my husband crazy. Sometimes, he once told me, he thought that I did it on purpose.

"What I asked was about your name, it sounds so familiar."

April smiled. She wondered how long it would take Nancy to connect the dots.

"I'm a writer," April told her.

"You can't be the same April Tanner," Nancy scoffed. "The horror fiction writer?"

"Guilty," she told her.

"Why, this is marvelous," Nancy said. "My friend, Mary, is going to be green with envy. Would you mind terribly if her and I, my friend and I, called on you sometime?"

"Anytime, Mrs. Jennings," April told her, if for anything to get another look at her tits.

"Wonderful," Nancy said, "and by the way, it is simply Nancy. Forget the damn conventional societal manners, love. I threw those things away a long time ago. Well, I must be going. I have so much to do today I dread even thinking about it. I would much rather stay and eat your pussy."

April started at the comment.

"I'm sorry?" April said.

Nancy paused before getting up from the sofa and said, "I said I would much rather stay and hear about your next book. Off again, dear?"

"I guess so," April told her but was damn sure that she had heard it right the first time.

Nancy let April open the front door before turning and offering a hand to her, saying, "Now if there is anything that you need, my number is taped to the cover of the casserole dish. Call me anytime, love."

April felt a slight squeeze from Nancy and thought that the woman had held her hand just a little too long before letting it go. With a wave, Nancy Jennings was down the steps and walking back up the street to her own house.

Closing the door, April stood for a long moment looking out the front room window, watching Nancy as she slowly made her way up the road. She watched as the lilt in her step seemed to be more exaggerated than need be, as if it were enticing April to call her back for a bit of sexual adventure. She bit her lower lip slightly and began to massage and fondle her own breasts. She could feel the yearning beginning again, wanting this stranger to come back and ravish her body.

"What the fuck?" April said aloud, realizing she was now masturbating to the woman down the lane.

She couldn't stop, bringing herself closer and closer to an orgasm. She closed her eyes and could imagine fucking the neighbor hard and long, running her hands across her body and tasting the sweat drenched skin. She rubbed herself furiously and let out a scream as she climaxed.

Looking around, she composed herself. She had masturbated before, even with John watching which seemed to turn him on more, but never had she experienced the intense orgasm that she had just experienced. It actually scared her a little but the feeling quickly wore away when she found herself wanting to do it again.

"Very good."

She turned to the sound of the soft whisper, the same voice that had been in her dream. Looking toward the fireplace, she saw the faint red glow coming from the stone.

Smiling, she removed her clothes, laid back down comfortably on the sofa, and began to explore her body again.

****

CHAPTER FIVE

"Fucking bitch!"

The music that was playing on the radio was not helping John's temper. It seemed to be making him madder as the pulsating rock rhythm pounded away on the vehicle stereo system. With what was almost a punch John turned off the infuriating sound. The only noise was now coming from the hum of the engine as he drove towards the outskirts of the town and up the winding road to his new home.

How dare she, he thought. He mused about the few times that either he or April had even had to discipline Bobby through any form of capital punishment. The one time that he did strike Bobby was only on the hand when the boy was two and was just about to topple over a boiling pot of spaghetti onto his head. Bobby had been so shocked that he did not even cry. He had only looked up at the tall man that he had called 'da' and listened at the admonishment that he was given.

He never reached for a hot pot again.

John slammed his hand onto the steering wheel, making it vibrate slightly. He imagined what would have happened had the teacher brought the authorities around. His brain began to invent all sorts of scenarios where Bobby was led away by clucking adults who knew how to raise other's children but had no children of their own and how he and April would be led in the opposite direction to a waiting patrol car, shackled in handcuffs.

His mind's eye invented the ensuing trial where he, John Tanner, noted scientist and husband to a successful author, screamed at the court and the judge that they were all incompetent fools. He saw himself leaping across the table at the bitch of a teacher, grabbing her around the neck and throttling her until her lying tongue protruded out of her mouth and her face turned a wonderful shade of red, then blue, and finally purple as the life drained away from her.

This last image made John smile for the first time since pulling away from the school. Yes, he could actually see the bulging eyes, the whimpering cries from the old cow as his hands tightened around her throat. He saw the pupils begin to dilate and the veins surrounding them popping with the onslaught of blood from the brain as it was deprived of the much needed oxygen. He smiled at how the tongue protruded and grew in size, its color turning greyer and greyer.

The honking of the horn brought him up short as he realized that he had nearly plowed into a pickup truck turning from the cross street. He had not even been aware of the red stop light and laid on his horn, throwing a finger out the window and yelling at the driver several vernaculars that previously he had been unaware of.

"Where did that come from?" he asked himself as he pulled into a parking lot. Putting the car into park, he realized that his hand was shaking and there was a thin film of sweat on his forehead. His heart was beating a little faster. His stomach was churning and he felt the need to vomit.

Looking out of the front windshield he saw the glowing red neon sign.

He smiled for the first time since leaving the school and he felt his anger subside. Naturally, he thought to himself, there had to be one in this small little town.

Stepping out of the car, he made his way towards the oaken door of Kelly's Bar.

It had been seven years since he had seen the inside of a bar and as he stepped in he was momentarily blinded by the sudden darkness. Closing his eyes he managed to get his bearings and waited for the nausea to pass. He was finally able to open his eyes again and in a moment they had finally adjusted to the low and subdued light of the bar. He looked around at the small place with its dozen or so tables and the long bar that stretched the length of the room. Behind it was what he could only assume was Kelly himself, wiping out glasses and putting them away.

John made his way to the center of the bar and sat on one of the stools. Reaching into his pocket, he pulled a twenty dollar bill from his wallet and laid it on the bar.

The bartender came over and asked, "What will you have?"

Licking his lips, John said in a low voice, "Whiskey, neat."

The bartender turned and grabbed a glass and the bottle of whiskey and poured the drink. He watched as John with a trembling hand raised the glass and downed the shot.

"Another?" the bartender asked.

"Just keep them coming," John said and downed the second shot. "At least until the twenty runs out."

The bartender poured another and waited to see if John would only sip or shoot it again. After satisfying himself that the man, his only customer at that point, was going to slow down a little, he placed the bottle of whiskey back in its place.

"Are you the owner?" John asked as he took a small sip of the alcohol.

"That would be me," the bartender told him.

"Then you must be Kelly," John said.

"No," the bartender told him as he began wiping out another glass, "that was the name of the bar when I bought it so I just left it that way. I'm Martin Adkins, sole proprietor of this wonderfully dead establishment."

"What do you mean dead?" John asked.

"Business has not been very good lately," Marty said. "I have tried everything from live bands, karaoke, even wet t-shirt contests, and nothing has helped. I'm thinking of selling the whole place and getting out of town."

John began to warm up to the whiskey, the turmoil in his stomach was beginning to settle and the confrontation had become only a nagging memory. He sipped at the drink again, letting the alcohol work magic in his body.

"I'm John Tanner," he told Marty. "My family just moved here and I guess I sort of stumbled onto the place."

"You want another shot?" Marty asked, noticing the empty glass.

"How about a beer," John said. "Whatever you have handy."

Marty reached into a cooler and opened a bottle, setting it in front John. John took a long swig, smacking his lips as he set the now half empty bottle down.

"You might want to go a little easy," Marty warned. "The cops in this town frown very deeply on people who drive under the influence. I should know, I used to be one of them."

"You were a cop?" John asked.

"Seventeen years before I got shot by some asshole with more gun than sense," Marty told him. "I was sort of forced into retirement due to the injury. The bullet hit my knee and pretty much shattered everything. They offered me a desk but I knew that I would never had survived doing paperwork, so I took early retirement, got full benefits, and bought this place. Every cops dream to own a bar, I guess."

"Now you are looking at getting rid of the place?" John asked, taking a smaller sip of beer.

"I guess I'm just getting tired of the small town life," Marty said with a sigh. "You mind if I join you?"

"Go ahead," John answered.

Marty took another beer from the cooler and set it beside John's before saying, "You see the same people come in, day after day, night after night, you hear the same old stories, and after a while, you feel like taking an axe and wiping them all out. You feel like you should bathe yourself in blood and listen to the screams as these assholes beg for their so called lives. Don't you think so?"

John was staring at the man behind the bar, not sure that he had heard him correctly.

"You can't just kill people like that," John said.

Marty looked at him with a strange smile and said, "Who said anything about killing? I just said that it gets a little boring hearing the same crap everyday and I wouldn't mind getting out of town. What did you think I said?"

John couldn't answer. Instead he said, "If you were to get rid of the place, how much would you want for it?"

"I'm not really sure, why, are you interested?" Marty asked.

"Well, we did just buy a house so I would have to look at the financial part of it," John began.

Marty smiled and took another swig of his beer. "Sounds more like the booze talking."

John laughed a little at the wise crack. He was beginning to feel much more relaxed and the scene with the teacher was now a fading memory that he could scarcely recall.

"You say you just bought a house here," Marty began, steering the conversation to another subject, "what part of town, if you don't mind my asking."

"Not at all," John answered. "A nice house up on something Bluff, I still don't have the names down yet."

Marty stopped short of taking another sip of his beer and set the bottle back down. His brow furrowed slightly as he said, "You mean Wilson's Bluff?"

"Yes, I think that is the name of the road," John said. "Why, do you know it?"

Marty wiped his lips with the back of his hand and all thoughts of selling the bar left his mind. "Mister, are you sure that you want to live up there?"

"Why do you say that?" John said, finishing the beer.

"Which house is it?" Marty asked.

"I think it is number 148, the first one that you get to after all of those damn curves," John told him.

"Yep, that's the one," Marty said and finished his own beer. Retrieving two more, he opened the bottles and set them onto the bar before saying, "Were you told everything about that place?"

"I suppose so," John said, "at least about the guy who killed himself while they were building it."

"Let me guess," Marty said, "Kendal sold it to you."

"Yes, that was the real estate agents name," John confirmed.

"Why, is there something that he didn't tell us? Are their bodies buried under the floor of the basement?"

"No, nothing like that," Marty told him. "I was a still a cop when that first family moved in two weeks after it was built. They were there for only about five days. Nice family, name of Bracket I think. Father, mother, two kids. I met them at the diner when they first hit town. Seemed to be really normal people, you know? Never found out what exactly happened but I do know the aftermath. I still get nightmares when I really think about."

John was intrigued and asked him what exactly did happen.

Marty took a long drink from his beer. "We got the call to go to the motel on the outskirts of town up by the highway. It seemed that someone had reported some strange noises coming from one of the rooms. To me, strange noises meant that there was some kind of orgy going on and they were getting a little too loud. I was the first on the scene. I will never forget that night as long as I live, and believe me I have tried.

"It was raining, real bad. I met the manager of the place outside under the portico and he showed me up to room 372 at the far end of the building. I could hear what they were complaining about fifty feet from the door. It was like some kind of animal screaming in pain. I pounded on the door as the manager stood a few feet away. The sounds inside just stopped and I got a shiver down my spine from the sudden silence. I knocked again and identified myself when the door opened. I looked in and drew my gun immediately."

"What did you see?" John asked in a low voice.

"This man, Daniel Bracket, whom I had just met a few days before, was naked, covered in blood, and I mean from his hair all the way down. The room was dripping with the stuff and what was left of his family was lying on the bed and the floor. In one hand he held a knife, and in the other he had the severed head of his wife. I told him to put the knife down and he just smiled at me. I told him not to do anything stupid and instead, he took the knife and cut deep into his throat, smiling the whole time as the blood spurted out of the wound. He was still smiling when he dropped to the floor. I can still hear the thud of the body and I still see that grin on his face as he died."

"Jesus," John muttered and took a long sip of his beer. He had read all of his wife's books and short stories, some which she had not even considered publishing because of the graphic content, but this made the nausea in his stomach return with a vengeance. He felt the mixture of the whiskey and the beer boiling inside, threatening to make a return engagement.

"You never found out why the guy had lost it?" John asked.

"Never did," Marty told him. "I even did a little investigating on my own. As far as we could tell, there was nothing going on in either his professional or personal life that would have warranted slaughtering his entire family. The funny thing was is that he did it at the motel. I figure it would have been easier to do it at the house."

"I'm glad he didn't do it at the house," John said, "Otherwise we might not have bought the place."

"Hope I didn't put you off of your new home," Marty told him. "That was never my intention, but I thought that maybe you might want to know."

"Thanks for telling me," John said, finishing his beer. "What do I owe you?"

Marty took the twenty and came back with change. "There was another owner shortly after, but from what I understand they only stayed one night. Young couple from what I was told that wanted to start a family."

"What happened to them?" John asked, standing up and stretching.

"Their car was hit by a tractor trailer," Marty said in a matter of fact voice. "Instantly killed was my understanding."

"Still," John said, "a little on the macabre side, wouldn't you say?"

"No more so than you chopping up your wife and son and having them for dinner," Marty said.

John looked up into the face of the bartender who looked completely normal.

"I'm sorry?" John said.

"I asked if you and your family had any plans for dinner." Marty said a little slower, thinking that John was not the brightest bulb on the chandelier.

"Oh," John said, "nothing that I know of. Why?"

"Another scheme to try and get business," Marty confided, "I know a little Mexican gal who is the greatest cook. I convinced her into coming in at least one night a week to cook up some authentic Mexican food. I have a full kitchen but no one to run it for me. I'm going to open the bar up for families until 9 tonight then it will have to be over 21 only. If you are interested, come on in."

John told him that he might take him up on the offer, making a mental note to see if April might be willing to go out tonight. As he left the bar, the sunlight hit him full force and he was once again blinded. At least the nausea had passed and he wasn't about to throw up on the sidewalk. A minute later, he was able to see and made his way to the car. Looking at himself in the rear view mirror, he realized how much that he had had to drink so early in the morning. He could already hear the admonishment that he would receive from his loving wife about not just falling off the wagon but taking a swan dive.

"Fuck it," he muttered as he started the car.

Bobby sat alone at the lunch table, staring at the hamburger, fries, and red apple that stared back at him. He heard the voices of the other children in the lunchroom, talking about the latest super hero movie or the funny video that someone had shared online. Being the new kid was hard and he felt self conscious being alone. He imagined the whispers and the fingers pointing at the kid who only stared at his plate of food. He could almost hear the jokes and the crude remarks about his clothes, his hair, or even the way that he walked alone down the halls. He wondered what they would say if he went into the kitchen area, picked up a knife and began slicing and dicing each and every one of them. He smiled at the thought of the screams and the pools of blood that some poor slob of a janitor would have to clean up.

"Hi."

The voice from across the table startled him and he looked up into the brown eyes of a girl. He blushed a little since he had never had a girl sit with him before. This was a whole new experience in the young life of Bobby Tanner and he was a little lost as to what to say.

She exaggerated the greeting again, her brown eyes wide and her lashes fluttering.

"Uh, hi," Bobby managed to work out of his mouth.

She pointed to the uneaten food and said, "It really isn't that bad if you use a lot of ketchup. Personally, I like mayo on mine but the school doesn't have any to just give out. I wind up having to bring my own."

She reached into her pocket and pulled a packet of mayo and proceeded to dress up her burger. "Want some? I have plenty."

"Um, no thanks," Bobby said. "I guess I'm not hungry. I had a big breakfast."

"I'm Gabby, sorry, Gabriella Henson," she told him, offering her hand which Bobby took and thought that it was the softest hand that he had ever felt. "You're the new kid."

"Bobby Tanner," he introduced himself to her.

"My friends call me Gabby for short but my mom thinks that it is improper for a young lady to use a shortened version of such a beautiful name," she said in a mocking tone.

"I think that it is a beautiful name," Bobby said and began to absentmindedly munch on the fries.

Gabriella was blond with big green eyes that seemed to sparkle when she spoke. To Bobby, she was the most beautiful ten year old girl that he had ever seen and he could feel something strange happening to his heart.

"So what do your parents do?" she asked. Before waiting for an answer she continued with, "My father works for the county as a fire fighter and my mom is head nurse at the hospital."

"Wow," Bobby muttered in awe.

"It's really no big deal," she continued between mouthfuls of burger, "nothing really ever happens in this town. That is why that as soon as I graduate, I'm going to college out west somewhere and get as far away from here as I possibly can."

"My dad is a scientist," Bobby told her, "he's not doing much of anything right now. I think he quit his job to be with mom and me a lot more."

"What does your mom do?" she asked.

"She writes," he told her.

"I read a lot, have I ever heard of her?" Gabby asked.

"Her name is April Tanner," Bobby told her and took a bite of hamburger without realizing it.

Those big green eyes widened in amazement and Gabby said, "Your mom is the April Tanner, the one that writes all of those horror books? My mom told me that I couldn't read any of her stuff because I was too young and wouldn't understand it. I told her that I was reading Poe and Shakespeare in the first grade and understood that. Anyway, as soon as she told me that I couldn't read it, I marched down to the library and read everything that they had on her. Gave me nightmares for a week, but it was well worth it."

"I will let her know," Bobby said, finishing the last of the burger. "She will take that as a great compliment."

"So how do you like the school?" Gabby asked.

"It's ok, I guess," Bobby said, staring into those green emeralds and becoming mesmerized.

"Hey, dork, why are you talking to her?"

The boy with the glandular problem that stood fifteen feet tall and six feet wide had bumped Bobby on the arm making him lose the last bite of burger. He had fiery red hair that looked liked it had been cut with a weed eater. His teeth were mostly stained but resembled that of a snarling wolf who has just met his latest prey.

"I said why are you talking to her?" the giant said.

"George, leave him alone," Gabby told the giant.

"Why do you want to sit with this geek?" George the giant asked her.

"Because I would rather sit with someone intelligent who can carry on an intelligent conversation than with an ape," she said which got a few snickers from neighboring tables.

"Oh yeah," George said, balling his fist tightly.

"Great comeback," Gabby said. "We cannot wait to hear your next syllable."

More laughter, and this time even Bobby snickered.

"What are you laughing at, dork head?" George glowered at Bobby.

Bobby could feel the anger somewhere deep in his stomach. This was not ordinary anger that people have when confronted for no reason. This was something very different, something that Bobby could not explain but knew that he liked the feeling. It seemed to be giving him power that he never thought that he had.

"Why don't you go fuck yourself," Bobby said slowly.

There was a collective intake of breath from everyone that heard it. Even Gabby looked shocked and her emerald eyes were even wider, seemingly covering her entire head.

"What did you say?" George said, now not feeling so tall anymore. Even he knew that the word that Bobby had just used was never to be spoken under threat of death and dismemberment by not only the school staff but by his parents. While he had heard his father say it on more than one occasion, he would never have repeated it.

Bobby stood up and realized that George was not much taller. His eyes squinted and his entire body tensed as he said, "I don't think that I was talking another language, or do you not understand English? I told you to go and fuck yourself. Go to whatever rock you crawled out from under, take the biggest knife that you can find and shove it as far up your ass as possible. Keep fucking yourself until there is nothing left of the asshole that you are."

The tension was over bearing as every child in the lunchroom within earshot didn't dare to breath for fear of missing this confrontation with the school bully and the new kid.

George tensed again, both fists balled so tight that the knuckles were turning white.

"Kid, you just made the biggest mistake of your short lived

life," George whispered through clenched stained teeth, his nose almost touching Bobby's nose as he leaned in close.

"No," Bobby said quietly, "you did."

Bobby's knee shot straight up into the groin of George the bully who crumpled to the floor in agony. His screaming brought on a collective gasp from the lunchroom.

"Mr. Tanner!"

Bobby turned quickly and saw the principle standing directly behind him.

"We do not condone this sort of behavior from our students," the principle said.

"It was George," Gabby told him, "he was the one that started it."

"Are you talking about George Wilkins who is currently sprawled on the floor in pain?" he asked the young girl.

"Bobby didn't want to do it but George was going to hit him, wasn't he Bobby?" Gabby said, attempting to diffuse the situation.

"Nevertheless, young lady, we cannot permit the kicking of other students, now can we," the principle said. Turning back to Bobby, he continued, "Mr. Tanner, I suggest that you go and sit in my office for a little while."

"Yes, sir," Bobby said. He looked over at Gabby and said, "Sorry."

The principle watched as the new kid walked out of the lunchroom and down the hall. Hearing the guttural groans coming from the floor, he looked down at George and said, "Oh, get up," before storming off.

George held onto his groin as he managed to stand. He looked at Gabby for perhaps sympathy and seeing that he wasn't going to get any from her, or anyone else, he vowed that somehow he would get even with the little dork.

"Honey, I'm home."

April lay on the sofa, her eyes staring up at the mantel. The soft red glow coming from the stone dimmed away to nothing as

John entered the house, bringing her out of whatever trance that she had found herself in. She raised herself up and greeted her husband as he came into the living room. She frowned a little when she smelled the distinct odor of alcohol on his breath.

"I thought that you said one glass of wine wouldn't hurt you," she said, her arms around his waist.

"So I had a drink, big deal," he said. "Besides, it was a good thing that I stopped at this place because we have been invited for an authentic Mexican dinner tonight."

"Wow," she said, kissing him on the cheek and feeling the familiar tingle between her legs. "I had a neighbor come over this morning and brought us a casserole. I guess we have our choice of what to do for dinner. We can have Mexican, casserole, or would you like me to finger my pussy and warm something up for you?"

John laughed and said, "After last night are you still horny?"

"You have no idea," April said, dropping to her knees and tugging at his belt.

"I thought that you might be a little upset with the drinking," he admitted to her.

Tugging at the belt and the zipper, she looked up at him and said, "Hell, if it makes you fuck better, drink the whole goddamn bar dry."

"What has got into you?" he asked as he felt her hand grabbing him and jerking his pants down.

"Hopefully you and this wonderful tool," she said and began teasing him with her lips and tongue.

"I've just never seen you this way, so forceful and oh my god," he managed to say before she engulfed him. Before he could even think about what he was doing, he grabbed April by the hair making her cry out slightly. Standing her up, he began to tear away at her clothes, exposing her body. With a lustful and almost evil leer, he forced her over the sofa and took her hard, making her cry out in an orgasm that seemed to last for hours. He pounded into her until he also climaxed, collapsing on the floor beside her.

"God, that was good," she told him as she slumped down beside him. "Drink more often."

"Stay horny more often," he told her. "So, do we go out tonight for Mexican or stay in for casserole?"

"Take me to the bedroom and fuck me again and then we can decide," she told him.

"Who are you and what have you done with Miss Conservative?" he asked her.

"She's taking a break for a while," April said. "I want to have some fun."

John smiled at his wife, but only for a moment. He wasn't sure at the time, but later would swear that he saw a glimmer of red somewhere deep within April's eyes. For just a split second, he thought that he was looking at another person, or another being, something that was made from pure hatred and lust, only to be replaced with the leering grin of his insatiable wife.

The afternoon was spent in the bedroom. John had never known his wife to be able to contort herself into so many positions. He couldn't believe that he was able to continue. The sex was more animalistic in nature and he felt her nails digging into his back and arms as she climaxed time after time. He felt her teeth sink into the soft flesh of his shoulder, causing him to wince in pain but not stopping the action. It was lucky that there had been a break in the sex as John looked at the bedside clock and realized that Bobby would be home any minute.

Quickly, they got dressed and waited for their son.

"So how was your day, big guy?" John asked Bobby.

Bobby walked into the house, laid his book bag on the sofa and collapsed in his father's favorite chair. He watched as his mother was unpacking the small bric a brac and odd books from a box and place them on the different shelves. He didn't answer his father, not really knowing how to tell him that he had gotten into a fight at school with some bully and had actually won, at least he thought that he had.

"It was ok, I guess," Bobby finally said. He was grateful that the phone would not be installed until the next day. At least the principle wouldn't be calling his parents about the incident.

"Nothing special happen today?" April asked.

"Just a typical day for the new kid in class," he told her. "What's for dinner?"

"Your father found a place in town that is doing authentic Mexican food and we were toying with the idea of going out tonight," April told him. "That is, if you are up for it."

"Sounds ok, I guess," he said. His voice sounded a little cold and distant but his parents didn't mention it. With a sigh he went to his room. Sitting at his desk he looked down at the blank piece of paper, his mind filling up with frightening images that demanded to be drawn. He closed his eyes tighter and tighter, trying to drive the pictures away from his imagination.

"You know you want to," the small voice inside of him said.

Yes, Bobby thought, he really did want to draw and paint. He felt that it was something that he was born to do.

He picked up a pencil and began to draw.

"It is all right if he goes with us, isn't it John?" April asked.

"Families are welcome up until nine so that would give us plenty of time," John told her. "Besides, I think that we could all use a little break from unpacking."

"Amen to that," April said and put the last book onto the bookshelf. Her eye caught the stone that lay on the mantle. A cold chill ran down her spine as she could have sworn that she had seen an actual eyeball deep within the stone, winking at her. It was something that she would never tell John about, a secret that she kept and would always keep from him.

"Did you feel that?" John asked and shivered slightly.

"What?" April said as she stretched her back.

"I'm not sure," he admitted. "It must have been a cold draft from the chimney, but it sure felt like someone just ran an ice cube down my spine."

"I didn't feel anything, just your hot tongue on my pussy," April told him.

"What did you just say?" John asked.

"I said that I didn't feel anything," she answered a little sternly. "What do you think that I said?"

John gave out a long sigh and said, "It isn't important. I have been hearing things all day. Guess that I am just a little tired from the moving."

April put her arms around him and held him tightly.

Bobby came walking into the living room slowly, watching the two embrace. Deep within him, he felt the urge to knock them both over, not in the playful way of wrestling like his father and him used to do when they lived in the apartment, but in a way that both of his parents would wind up with broken necks, blood gushing from their mouths as their heads met the floor, their skulls crushed deeply until the bone fragments entered into their brains. The thought made him smile and he remembered the look of pain on the bully's face at school.

"Are we going out, or what?" Bobby asked.

"Yes, big guy," April said, releasing her husband, "we are leaving very shortly."

"Great," he said, "I'm starving."

"Then let us remove ourselves from this humble abode and proceed to the establishment which promises to satiate us all," John said in a regal tone which made his wife laugh. "Please, my lady, our carriage awaits yonder in the courtyard."

Even Bobby's thoughts of blood and death were pushed aside and he laughed aloud saying, "Dad, you are silly."

With a deep bow, he motioned his family toward the front door. As he stood up, he saw the small flicker of red coming from the stone out of the corner of his eye.

Martin showed the family to the rear table personally. He took the orders and delivered the food himself, waiting patiently for anything else that the Tanner's might need.

"No waiters tonight?" John asked.

"Of course not," he answered, "Not that we would need any. Look around this place, Mr. Tanner. You are my third customer for this extravaganza. I told you, it doesn't matter what the hell I do in here, no one comes. I'm about ready to chuck the whole thing and move to Florida."

"By the way," John began, "I would like you to meet my wife, April and this is our son, Bobby."

"The food is very good," April told him which at least brought a small smile to his face.

"Thank you very much," Martin said. "If there is anything that I can do for you, as you can see, I have plenty of time."

"Are you serious about selling the place?" John asked.

"Were you serious about buying me out?" Martin said.

"John," April said, "you don't know anything about running a bar, except how to drink in one, which I thought that you had stopped."

"I only had a couple of beers," John told her, feeling the tightness around his jaw. "Can we discuss it when we get home?"

"Sure you don't want to have a couple of more for the road?" April asked her voice low and hateful.

"I will just be over by the bar," Martin told them and made a hasty retreat, not wanting to see the fight that he was sure was about to ensue.

"Dammit, April, what the hell is wrong with you?" John said, slamming a fist onto the table. "I said that we will discuss it when we get home."

"Maybe we will and maybe we won't," April told him through clenched teeth. "You promised me that you were done and for the past seven years you have been wonderful. What the hell happened that made you take a drink."

"You didn't seem to mind it earlier," he told her, thinking back to the rough sex.

"That is not fair," April said hurtfully.

"Let's just enjoy the meal," John said.

Bobby had been watching closely, slowly eating the burrito and drinking the soda that he had ordered. Somewhere, deep within his eyes, there was a glowing red light, and it was very happy.

The fight had been very loud and very long. Bobby had been sent to his room the minute that they had walked into the house.

April had started in on John's drinking and John had countered with the fact that he may have to hire a stunt cock to come in and please her while he got some rest. This brought on a barrage of expletives from April and the fact that if John had a bigger dick that she may just be satisfied.

The two had separated for about an hour after that, April running in tears to the bedroom and John sitting in his chair in the living room. He listened to the sobs from his wife and his heart grew heavy. He wasn't sure what the hell was going on with the family. He wasn't sure what the hell was going on with him. He had never even thought about drinking before the first night in the house when they toasted with a bottle of wine. Now he was going into a bar and knocking back a few that would have put him on his ass a few years ago.

Slowly, he stood up and headed for the bedroom. He no longer heard April crying, only moaning softly.

"April?" he called out softly as he approached the bedroom door.

There was no answer, only the sounds of his wife breathing heavily. He slowly opened the door and was taken aback at what he saw.

April was naked, lying on the bed, furiously rubbing herself to the point where the skin had turned raw and was beginning to bleed. She opened her eyes and looked at her husband, her smile almost cruel and inhuman as she lifted her hand toward her mouth and began to lick and suck the index finger.

John ran to her before she could do anymore. Shaking her violently, he slapped her once on the cheek.

April, shocked that John had actually hit her, began to cry again. She curled up into his arms and after a moment was sound asleep.

John gently laid her on the bed and covered her naked form with a blanket. Still fully dressed, he nestled beside his wife and passed out.

John and April stood before the fireplace, hand in hand. On the mantel, the stone had seemed to grow to the size of a football with a glowing red eye in the center. The entire room was bathed in the red glow.

John tried to force himself to look away from the evil thing, for he knew almost instinctively that it was pure evil from somewhere in the depths of hell. No matter what he tried, he couldn't turn from the glowing red eye. He could hear some sort of humming sound coming from all around him. His grip tightened around April's hand as if he thought that she would slip away from him and fall into a deep and dark chasm. He felt her hand tighten also and this gave him a little comfort, knowing that she was still there.

The light became more and more intense, pulsating with a demonic rhythm that grew louder and louder. The sound had become so intense that John could feel the small veins in his ears beginning to burst. He could feel the blood running down his neck.

With a great deal of effort, he managed to turn his head toward April.

April smiled, still wearing the sheer nightgown that she had put on earlier in the evening. She let go of his hand and walked in front of him, the large stone and glowing eye behind her. She took off the nightgown and stood naked before him, running her hands up and down her body, her eyes closed. She opened them again and reached out for John, taking off his clothes seductively. Her tongue ran across her lips as she began to fondle him.

John was both horrified and mesmerized by the sheer sexual nature that his wife was displaying. He wasn't sure what was happening but it was definitely awakening a passion deep within him. He wanted her with every fiber of his soul. He found himself hardening with her ever increasing strokes. He looked behind her and saw the stone growing larger, the eye growing more intense.

He grabbed at April and forced himself deep inside her, making her scream with passion. He began to thrust harder and harder into her. He expected to feel her nails digging into his back, drawing blood. Instead, he closed his eyes and began to pump harder and harder into her.

When he opened his eyes again, he saw the look of pain on her face. He could not understand the look but continued to thrust into her. He then noticed why he had not felt her caressing hands on his back. As he climaxed, his breathing coming in short gasps, he looked and saw that his wife, the woman that he had loved for many years, had been shackled. Each wrist was bound with a chain that went to nowhere but remained taut. Each ankle was strapped and held her in a spread eagle position.

John fell backwards, landing hard on the floor, his wife shackled directly above him. He noticed the thin red line that had begun just above her pubic area. It seemed to be traveling up her abdomen and in between her breasts. Looking behind her, he noticed that the stone was now the size of the entire fireplace, replacing the wall and glowing more intently that John was unable to stare into the brilliant light.

He looked back up at his wife and saw that the thin line was now beginning to open. Blood poured from the crevice as the chains holding her began to pull her apart.

"John, please help me," April screamed as the crevice widened, spilling her intestines and blood onto him. With a final jerk, her body was torn in half. Her head fell into John's lap, still mouthing the words.

John was frozen in terror. Blood and gore covered him and the floor. He looked down at the head of his wife staring back up at him with milky white eyes. Her severed head began to laugh with a maniacal glee.

John woke up screaming.

His breath came in short bursts and he expected April to be there, holding him closely, telling him that it had only been a dream.

He looked over to the other side of the bed.

The corpse looked back at him, screaming and laughing.

Again, John woke up still screaming in deathly fright. This time he looked to see that April was indeed no longer in the bed.

"April?"

There was no sound coming from anywhere in the house. He glanced at the clock on the bedside table.

Two in the morning.

He got out of the bed and made his way toward the living room, stopping long enough to check on Bobby who would have surely heard the cries of his father.

Bobby lay peacefully asleep in his own room.

Making his way toward the living room, he called out again for his wife, only to be met with the silence of the house.

He found her on the sofa, naked and spread eagle, facing the fireplace, as if awaiting a long lost lover.

"April?" he called out again.

She turned to him and for a brief moment, he thought that he caught a small flicker of red somewhere deep within her eyes.

He reached out toward her and with a sudden movement; she bit into his arm deeply. He raised his hand to strike her for the second time that evening but stopped as she let him go, went limp and collapsed back onto the sofa, whimpering like a small child.

He managed to pick her up and carry her back to the bedroom, only glancing up to the fireplace mantel hoping that he would not see a giant stone with a red eye in the center of it. Placing April back onto the bed, he covered his wife again before going into the bathroom and treating the bite on his arm. Small trickles of blood began to ooze from the teeth marks, running into the sink. Splashing cold water onto his arm, he splashed more onto his face and looked into the mirror.

He cringed at the face that looked back at him. It seemed to have aged years in only one night.

Somehow, he was able to crawl back into bed and fall into a restless sleep.

****

CHAPTER SIX

"I think that maybe we should frame it."

April was looking at the small stone on the mantel as John came from the kitchen, a piece of toast in his hand. He was almost afraid to look up at the mantel for fear of what he might see. It took a few moments, but he was at last able to look and only saw the small stone that his son had found.

"What do you mean frame it?" he asked April.

"I don't know," she admitted, "maybe something like a shrine for it. You know, you did tell Bobby that it was here to protect the house and all who occupied within."

"Yes I remember," he assured her. "Why would you want to make a shrine out of it?"

"I really don't know," she said absently. Looking back at John, she noticed the bandage on his arm.

"John, what happened?" she asked with concern.

"Oh, nothing," he said, trying to play it off.

"Well something happened to you, and obviously it happened last night," she said a little sternly.

"There was a dog trying to get in when I came down for a late night snack," he lied.

"A dog?" she asked. "I may assume from the bandage that it bit you."

"It's really nothing," John said. "I thought I might stop by the doctor's office and have him take a quick look at it."

"I'm just thinking about rabies," she told him.

"Believe me honey," he began, "being a scientist I have thought of little else since last night."

"I just can't believe that you didn't wake me up," she told him.

"I can't believe that with that much noise I didn't wake up at all. You know what a light sleeper I can be."

"Yes, I know," he said and caught the stone in the corner of his eye.

"Promise me you will get it looked after," she said.

"Yes my love, I will get it looked at," he told her. "I have to go to Atlanta today anyway and pick up some supplies. I thought I might stop in and see Stan at the lab."

"I take it you will not be home for dinner," she said flatly. "I know you and Stan Fielding. He will probably talk you into having dinner with him and whatever little hot blonde that he is dating now and then you two will start talking shop and god knows when you will be home."

"I promise you dear that nothing like that will happen. If I leave now I may have lunch but that will be it."

She gave him a knowing glare and then smiled.

"Well, I thought I might go into town and stock up the bar for you," she said. "At least when you get home you can have a martini."

"I will call and let you know when I start back," he told her.

She ran her tongue across her lips and began to stroke him through his pants.

"Why don't I give you something to come back for," she said as she slowly dropped to her knees.

It didn't take long for him to climax and watch his wife stand up and head for the kitchen. Thank God that Bobby had already gone to school. He decided before leaving to see if Bobby had done any more drawings. He made his way up to the bedroom and went immediately to the small desk. What greeted his eyes was something that made his stomach turn. He picked up the picture and folded it carefully, placing it into his pocket. Heading back down the stairs he made sure that April was still in the kitchen.

"Hey lover," she said. She had been wearing a skirt and t-shirt. Now she was bent over the sink, the skirt raised above her waist, exposing herself to him. "See anything you like?"

"Honey, I really need to get going," he told her, trying to ignore the aching in his groin.

She wiggled her ass at him and smiled. "Are you sure?"

No, dammit, he wasn't sure of anything anymore.

John walked up to his wife, unzipping his pants for the second time that morning. The sex was quick and hard but strangely not very satisfying. She turned afterwards and kissed him hard before heading toward the basement.

Walking toward the front door, he turned and saw the stone on the mantel. Quietly, he took a cloth from the kitchen and grabbed the stone, wrapping it up and placing it into his pocket before heading out the door.

April sat before her computer, a blinking cursor mocking her, daring her to write a cohesive sentence. Since moving into the house she had had only one thing on her mind and it was beginning to frighten her. It seemed that a lot of things were beginning to frighten her and she could not explain any of them. She almost felt as if she were living one of her stories.

While sex had always been great with John, lately she could think of nothing else. Sometimes her fantasies did not even include her husband and she wasn't sure whether to be annoyed with that or excited by it. Even now while staring at the computer screen, her right hand was beginning to rub her groin lightly as if trying to coax her into another marathon session of self gratification.

She heard the car start up and drive away. For a moment, she felt as if a weight had been lifted off of her shoulders. She shuddered slightly and looked back at the computer. Smiling, her fingers began to dance along the keyboard as her mind conjured up a story that was even giving her chills.

Three hours later, she found herself still sitting in front of the computer, typing furiously.

****

CHAPTER SEVEN

The drive down I-75 was pleasant for John. Normally he would have had the air conditioner running as he cruised along with the traffic. Instead, he had opted for open windows and the wind blowing his hair around his eyes. The radio was playing classic rock and he was singing along with Jefferson Airplane and Led Zeppelin, his fingers drumming the steering wheel. He found himself more relaxed than he had been since moving into the house.

His mind conjured up the dream from the night before. The bite on his arm was beginning to throb with a dull ache again, but even that did not bother him.

He found the lab parking lot where he used to work and made his way past the security check points to the lab of Dr. Stan Fielding, now the head of the department when John vacated.

"Anything going to blow up in here?" he asked as he entered the area.

"It's about goddamn time you came back here," Stan said without looking up from the microscope that he was peering into.

"You must really love my job," John said as he pulled up a stool beside his friend.

Stan looked up and almost recoiled in surprise.

"What the hell happened to you?" Stan asked. "You look like something out of the grave."

"Actually I feel better than I look," John told him although he knew better.

"I would hope so," Stan told him. "You looked like you have aged ten years since the last time I saw you. I thought the mountain air was supposed to be good for you. Looking at you I will take the smog of the city any day."

"I don't think that it's the air doing it. Besides, can't an old friend drop in to say hi every once in a while?"

"Now just hold it right there," Stan said. "You decide to leave this wonderful place to basically live off of your wife who by the way is sorely missed to do some sort of research on your own, leaving me with the glamorous job of head of the department at a substantial raise and you expect me to believe that you just dropped in to say hi? Don't try to shovel it on me, buddy boy."

"I take it that you really love my job?" John asked.

"What's not to love?" Stan answered sarcastically. "Double the work load, fighting with the old man upstairs over budgets and why hasn't this experiment been completed or trying to explain to a drug company that the results that they wanted aren't what they are getting, yes, in answer to your question I really love my job."

There was a slight pause before Stan said, "When are you coming back?"

John laughed.

"Believe me, Stan; I have no intention of giving up country life to come back here."

"Just thought I would ask," Stan said grinning. "So why did you come?"

"Like I said, I just stopped in to say hi," John reiterated.

"Now look," Stan said firmly, "I am a highly paid scientist working on twenty different experiments at this very moment. You would not have driven the three hours it takes to get here through the traffic from hell just for a friendly visit."

"All right," John finally admitted. He pulled the cloth from his pocket and laid it on the counter in front of his friend. Carefully he unfolded it to reveal the stone. "Tell me what this is."

Stan looked down and then looked up at John and said, "It's called a rock. That will be $7,000 consultation fee."

"I know it's a rock, smart ass. I want to know what kind of rock."

"Damn dirty one, I can tell you," Stan continued. "Now it's up to 8 grand."

"Keep it up and I will come back to work," John told him.

"All right, let me see it," Stan said and started to reach for it.

John grabbed his arm to the surprise of Stan.

"Hey, I need to pick it up, don't I? What the hell is the matter?"

"Sorry," John said, releasing Stan. "I don't know to tell you the truth."

Stan rolled his eyes and reached for the stone again. He jerked back and grabbed his finger.

"What happened?" John said with concern.

"The damn thing bit me," Stan said and examined his index finger. There was a small droplet of blood forming at the end of it.

"Maybe there was a bug on it," John tried for a feeble explanation.

"Great," Stan said, "first you bring in a filthy rock into my nice clean lab and now you're telling me that there may have been a bug on it. Now how am I supposed to explain to the old man upstairs the expenditure of sterilizing this room again when we just had it done yesterday?"

"Sorry," John said.

"Let's try this again," Stan said and picked up the stone without incident. He felt the smooth surface, noticing the small scratches on each side. He turned it over in the palm of his hand several times before placing it back onto the table.

"Well?" John asked.

"Like I said, it's a rock."

"Can you at least run some sort of test on it to find out what kind of rock?" John asked exasperated.

"Hey man, calm down a little," Stan told him with concern. "I can do that, no problem. It's going to take a couple of hours. Why don't we go and get something to eat. I'm buying."

"Yea," John said, calming down a little. "I guess I am a bit hungry."

"I'll get the test started and then we can go out."

The medium well steak that John had ordered tasted better than anything that he had partaken of in recent memory. The baked potato, slathered in butter and sour cream, and the salad had both been equally enjoyable. He found himself relishing every bite, savoring the tender meat. It was as if he had eaten steak for the very first time. He was carefully cutting into the meat, taking small portions, hoping that the meal would never end.

"Looks like you are enjoying yourself," Stan commented, biting into his own prime rib.

"Do you eat this good for lunch every day?" John asked between mouthfuls. "Did the old man increase the meal allowance?"

"The answer to both of those questions is no," Stan told him. "I just thought that since you graced me with your presence I would treat you to an extravagant lunch."

"I will not sleep with you," John quipped.

"Damn, and here I thought I was making progress," Stan retorted.

Both men laughed.

"I also noticed that you opted for the red wine," Stan said. "Diving off the wagon?"

"It's funny," John said, looking at the untouched glass of wine, "I don't know why I ordered it. I don't really want it."

"Waitress," Stan called out. "Would you bring my friend a glass of your finest soda? I believe he prefers Coke over Pepsi."

The waitress smiled and returned a minute later with the drink, taking away the wine.

"Better?" Stan asked.

John sipped at the cool beverage, noticing that even it tasted remarkably good. He smiled and dived back into his steak.

"So how are things up north?" Stan said.

For the first time since starting the meal, John paused. He laid his fork and knife down, wiped his mouth with the cloth napkin, and almost broke down and cried.

"Stan," John began after composing himself, "I don't know where to begin. We have only been in the house a couple of days and it's like my family is falling completely apart."

"Give me a for instance," Stan said.

"Ok, let's start with me. You said yourself that I have looked like I have aged ten years. Believe me, I feel like I have. One day after being in that house, I thought I might kill a school teacher who was simply showing concern for Bobby. I didn't just fall off the wagon, I took a swan dive so hard that I was seriously considering buying a bar, and on top of everything else, I am having the most horrible dreams."

"What is going on with Bobby?" Stan asked, no longer interested in his own meal and giving full attention to his friend.

John sighed and said, "You remember the sort of drawings and paintings he would do."

"As I recall he is somewhat of a prodigy."

"Exactly, years ahead of his time," John continued. "Well, his work has taken on a sort of darkness; I'm not sure how to describe it. He would draw such happy pictures of landscapes and incredible portraits that almost seemed lifelike. Here," John said as he reached into his pocket and pulled out the drawing that he had found that morning. "Take a look for yourself."

Stan took the folded paper and opened it, recoiling slightly at the grotesque picture.

"What the hell is it?" Stan asked.

"You tell me," John said.

Stan looked again. It was a solid dark circle with three stick figures in the middle, an obvious representation of the family. Above the circle was a giant red eye, bloodshot and evil, looking down on the stick family. Stan felt a shiver run up and down his spine as he looked at the eye.

"You're sure that Bobby drew this?" Stan asked. "As I recall, he never drew stick figures before."

"I found that on his desk this morning just before I left," John said.

"I can see why you are concerned," Stan said, handing the picture back to John. "What else is going on?"

"Well, the tension is so high you need an aqualung to breathe," John said. "April has transformed into some hyperactive nymphomaniac that I'm seriously considering putting her in the porn industry!"

Stan's eyes widened as he said, "And how is that a bad thing?"

"No, Stan, you don't understand. Our sexual life was fine, not routine but very good. We actually made love to each other and enjoyed ourselves. Even after Bobby was born we still could copulate with the best of them. Now, it is like a frenetic pace of constant sex. There is no emotion involved, only the physical act. Believe me, I am a very obliging lover but I don't think that I will be able to afford the medical expenses."

"What do you mean?"

"April could become intense at times, holding onto my back or arms, even digging her nails into my back. I don't mind the scratching, but these were deep, drawing blood."

Stan tried to soak it all in, analyzing the situation that his friend now found himself in. "So what do you think is going on?"

"That's just it, I don't have the faintest idea," John admitted. "At first I thought it might have something to do with the house itself. You've seen the movies and read the books."

"You don't actually believe in any of that, do you? We both are highly trained and respected scientists. There has not been one piece of actual scientific evidence to support any supernatural findings of any kind. You know that!"

"Yes Stan," John said, "I know that. I also know that there are many things that science has yet to explain. We can hypothesize all day long but the fact remains that strange things do happen in this big world of ours that cannot be explained away. All I was saying was that perhaps there is something very wrong with the house and it is affecting me and my family."

"So you are talking about a possible toxic explanation, some sort of gas emitting from somewhere," Stan said. "Now something like that I can deal with. Have you had any tests done?"

"Not yet," John said. "It's only been a couple of days since we moved in. I was going to check into having that done later today or possibly tomorrow."

Stan looked at his watch and said, "Well, the rock test should be about finished. Let's go check it out."

Stan was studying the computer readout and frowning. John was sitting next to him looking at the computer screen. Both men looked at each other.

"Damndest thing that I have ever seen," Stan said and began pointing to different places on the graph that was presented to them. "You see here, there are all the normal elements, quartz, limestone, even small flecks of gold, but this one is the one that puzzles me."

"The highest element, the highest point on the graph and all that the computer can say is that it is an unknown substance," John said.

"Could you leave that stone with me for a couple of days?" Stan asked. "I can mail it back to you. I have a friend at the lab across town and they have a bigger system for things like this. Maybe they could give me some answers."

"Sure, keep it for as long as you need it," John told him, still looking at the puzzling graph on the screen.

"I will take it over there this afternoon and when they get done I will mail it back to you," Stan told him as they made their way toward the front doors.

"Or you could drive it up to us," John offered. "I know that April would love to see you. Maybe you could coax one of those hot lab assistance to come with you for the weekend. That is unless you have finally met that certain someone?"

"I meet that certain someone almost every day," Stan said and laughed. "You know that I am completely against the institution of marriage."

"The quintessential confirmed bachelor," John told him. "You know that all of that dating and partying is going to catch up to you one day."

"Give my love to April," Stan said as John exited the building and headed for his car.

Stan watched his friend cross the parking lot. He turned and headed back to the lab, thinking about the way life used to be when his friend was also his boss. The lab seemed to run better, smoother before John had decided to leave. Stan wasn't angry at being promoted, in reality he had hoped that he would get the promotion and the responsibility that had come with it.

Stan made a slight detour to the men's room. Looking at himself in the mirror, he marveled at how well he did look for his age. Going on his mid forties he still had all of his auburn hair, he was still in decent shape, working out three times a week, and he had not developed the middle age paunch in his stomach. All in all, he admitted that he was a very handsome man.

"You're still lonely," he told his reflection.

It wasn't that he had not been on dates, but recently the caliber of women that he was meeting was not exactly up to standards. They would be great in bed but then they would begin to talk, he thought to himself. While he wasn't expecting to meet a rocket scientist he expected them to at least know what two plus two was.

Washing his hands, he noticed the dull throb in his finger. Raising it up for closer inspection, he saw the small black spot where the stone had apparently bit him. It was as if infection had set in while he was having lunch. Shrugging, he made his way back to the lab.

He saw the stone on the table and blinked. He wasn't sure, but he swore that he had seen it glowing slightly under the brilliant florescent lights of the lab. It was a soft red glow that seemed to pulsate like that of a heartbeat. He approached the stone slowly, not looking away for fear that the light would wink out. As he picked up the stone he noticed that it was warm, almost too hot to touch. He placed it into a small box, made a copy of the report findings from the computer, and decided to take the stone to his friend at the other lab.

As he got into his car, a feeling of foreboding gripped him and he shuttered uncontrollably. He imagined that he could almost feel the pulsating light emitting from the stone inside the box that lay on the seat beside him. It was a feeling that something was very wrong and he could not shake it.

Starting the car, he left the lab parking lot and headed across the city.

****

CHAPTER EIGHT

The trees along the two lane highway seemed greener to John since leaving the stone with his friend and associate. The sun shone a brilliant yellow orange in the sky high above the speeding car and John did not even feel bothered by the heat. He had rolled the windows down and was letting the wind whip his hair around his face, reveling in the feel of it as it brushed across his eyes. He found himself humming something from Three Dog Night, a song that he had not thought about in a long time.

He reached over and turned on the radio and tuned to a classic rock station. He patted the wheel with the palm of his hands in time to the music. Reaching over to the radio, he turned it up to its fullest volume, filling the car with the music. He found himself smiling and singing along to Aerosmith, Led Zeppelin, The Eagles, and even Bob Seger, hitting the high notes a little off key but not caring. He would laugh at how his voice would strain to reach the higher pitches, thinking to himself that he had least tried to match the classic singers from the past.

Traffic was light and he was making great time. He wasn't sure what had made him take the alternate route home, bypassing the major interstate for the two lane highway. Perhaps it was the feeling that he had, as if he had woken from a nightmare and was now analyzing the dream, telling himself that it had all just been a nasty dream that his mind had conjured up for his sleeping brain. The feeling of relief had so overwhelmed him that he was unaware of anything except the beautiful blue sky, the green trees, the yellow sun…

The flashing red and blue lights in his rear view mirror brought him up short and he slowly began to pull over to the side of the road. Even the act of being caught by a state highway patrol officer did nothing to diminish his mood. He quickly took out his wallet and removed the license, placing it on the dashboard in front of him. He looked into the rearview mirror and watched the officer slowly walk up to the car, check the license plate on the rear before approaching the driver's window with caution.

"Afternoon, sir," the officer said.

John giggled a little, catching himself quickly.

The officer frowned a little but continued with, "Do you realize how fast you were going?"

John began to laugh harder.

"Sir, have you been drinking?" the officer said, stepping back cautiously.

"No, but I will join you if you are buying!" John said and laughed even harder. He couldn't control the guffaws that were emitting from his mouth. He looked at himself in the mirror and saw the almost maniacal expression on his face as he continued to laugh.

"Sir, why don't you step out of the car," the officer politely said.

John unhooked his seatbelt, opened the door, looked at the officer, and fell to the pavement in another wave of hysterical laughter.

"Sir, how much have you had?" the officer said, reaching for his shoulder radio to call for back up.

After a moment, John was able to get himself under control. Slowly, he stood up and managed to hand the officer his driver's license.

The officer reached out and slowly took the document, looking at it carefully.

"Is everything all right, Mr. Tanner?" the officer asked.

"You will have to excuse me, officer," John began, "I'm sorry for the laughter. I suppose I was speeding and I sincerely apologize. I guess I just wasn't paying attention to what I was doing. As for the laughing, well, I guess I'm just in a very happy mood. Whatever ticket you need to write, please do so and I will be more than happy to pay it."

The officer was taken aback. In all of the stops that he had made in his ten year career as a patrol officer, he had never stopped anyone that not only was willing to admit guilt but was downright happy about it. He scratched his head, told John to wait by the car and headed back to his own car to fill out the paper work.

John felt the uncontrollable urge to laugh again but managed to hold it in. The officer returned and informed him that he had been driving seventeen miles over the speed limit. The ticket was not an admission of guilt and there was a court date listed if he would like to have a trial. Otherwise, there was an address where he could mail a check for the fine which was listed at the bottom of the ticket.

After John signed the ticket, the officer let him go.

Yes, John thought as he drove on being a little more careful to watch the speedometer, things were looking up. Perhaps he would be able to get some sleep tonight.

After the quickie with John and shortly after he had left to see his friend and colleague, April had walked past the mantel heading for the basement and her own writing space. She turned and frowned as she stared at the place where the stone should have been.

She looked around, thinking that perhaps Bobby had taken it to school or it had fallen off and rolled under the sofa. After a few minutes of searching, the earnestness to find the thing had left her. It was no longer all that important to find the stone and replace it on the mantel.

Instead, she made her way to try and pick up where she had left off on her new novel.

Thinking for only a moment, her fingers began to fly across the keyboard. The story was coming alive again and she could see in her mind's eye the action that she was typing out. The characters became fuller and more complete for her as the situations that she was setting them in became real for her. Her fingers could hardly keep up with what her mind was producing.

After what seemed to her was only about a half hour, she stretched and looked at the clock and blinked. Somehow, she had been working for almost five hours straight. Her fingers had stiffened slightly from the exertion but the product had been quite exhilarating. She scanned over the text and with a satisfied grin she thought that perhaps she could finish the latest book by next week if she kept up this kind of pace. Saving the work and making a back up copy on a separate flash drive, she closed the program and turned off the computer.

"Wow," she thought to herself as she climbed the stairs to the living room. She thought that perhaps she would make something very special for dinner. Walking to the kitchen, she rummaged around at the groceries, picking up cans of vegetables and pulling out some chicken from the freezer. It would be a spectacular meal, complete with candles and perhaps some soft music. She was proud of her culinary skills and wanted to show off after completing four new chapters of her latest work of fiction.

She checked the time and noticed that Bobby would be home from school, possibly wanting a snack before dinner. She also wanted to make sure that she had enough time to dress up for her wonderful husband who would be arriving back just about the time that the dinner would be completed. She mentally took note of the closet and picked out a soft silk red dress that she had not worn in a long time. She smiled at the lustful look that John had given her the first time that she had worn it.

"Hi mom," Bobby said as he came bounding through the front door. "Look what I did today!"

"I'm in the kitchen, honey," she called out.

Bobby ran in, his book bag thrown onto the kitchen floor, waving a large piece of paper in the air. For the first time since moving into the house, Bobby was actually in a good mood.

"What do you have there?" April asked, taking the paper. Looking at it her face broke into a huge grin. "This is quite good, young man."

Bobby beamed.

The drawing was of the front of the school, but not the kind that a child would draw. The depiction had almost intricate details, right down to the leaves on the trees that lined the walkway. Bobby had even drawn students walking along the front, carrying books and smiling.

"My teacher says that I show great improvement with my drawings," he told her. "She wants that one back so that she can display it and I told her that I would have to let you and dad decide."

"Let's wait for your father to get home and we can discuss it over dinner," she said and placed the drawing on the refrigerator with a magnet. "I'm sure that he will agree, as long as we get it back."

"She only wants it for a few days," Bobby said. "When is dinner?"

"In a couple of hours," she answered him and returned to the stove. "Your father should be home soon. Would you like to go outside and wait for him?"

Without a word, Bobby headed out the door.

"That's my young man," April said aloud. Checking the oven and making sure that everything was set she went to the living room and created a makeshift table. Placing candles around the room and finding the perfect music, she went upstairs to get dressed.

"Hey big man!"

John called out to his son who was sitting on the front lawn, doing what he always did. He wasn't the kind of boy that ran around or climbed trees, but instead stared at the sky and created pictures from the clouds that formed. He had a small sketchpad and was busy creating from his imagination pictures of animals and faraway kingdoms, dragons and creatures that had no name. He was surely in his own world.

John parked the car and headed inside.

As he walked in, he felt relieved. He wasn't sure what to

expect since a feeling of dread had descended on him ever since they had moved in two days ago. How could something like that happen in such a short space of time? Now, he thought for the first time this was indeed their home. The home that both April and he would live out their lives in, grandchildren playing on the same lawn that Bobby was sitting on now.

He looked around and saw the table that April had set up. Candles illuminated the room, casting a warm glow that fully established his feeling of being at home. The red glow from the stone in his nightmare was only a distant memory now.

"Hello lover," April said.

John's mouth dropped open. She was standing in the doorway across the room, posing seductively in the red dress. Her hair and makeup were perfect and she was smiling at him in that way that always drove him wild.

Crossing the room, John took her into his arms and kissed her long, softly exploring her mouth with his tongue.

"Hello," he said as he pulled away slightly from the embrace.

"Would you like a drink before dinner?" she asked.

"Actually," he began, "I don't think so. Look, I stumbled off the wagon for a couple of days but right now, I think just a soda will do."

"I was hoping that you would say that," April said as she made her way to the kitchen. "Can you call Bobby in for dinner?"

As Bobby came in, April had put the last of the meal onto the table. The family sat down and began to talk, really talk. April was excited about the new chapters, Bobby was telling his father about the new drawing, and even John explained about the traffic stop. At first, April was concerned that he had been stopped but realized that John was not concerned at all and her feelings of happiness returned. It was a scene of peaceful domesticity.

After dinner, the entire family cleaned up the living room. Bobby helped his mother with the dishes as John arranged the furniture again. They all sat down with a large bowl of popcorn, heavily buttered and salted, and found a movie that they would all enjoy on the television. Bobby fell asleep halfway through it and carefully, John carried him upstairs to the bedroom, tucking him in and kissing him on the cheek.

Returning to his wife, they cuddled and watched the end of the movie.

"You are one terrific lady," John told her as he brushed an errant hair from her face.

"You are pretty terrific yourself, man," she said, softly stroking his arm. "I hope that you won't get mad at me."

"After that dinner?" he exclaimed. "What could I be mad about?"

"Do you think that maybe we could lock up, go upstairs, take off our clothes, climb into bed, and just cuddle?"

"No sex tonight?" he asked.

"I just want to feel your arms holding me," she said softly, gently kissing him on the cheek. "I want to look into your eyes and feel your body next to mine, keeping me warm. I just want you to hold me all night and let me fall asleep in your arms."

"I believe that it can be arranged," he told her, smiling and kissing her gently on the lips.

"I just don't want to see any red lights tonight, or have any nightmares," she confessed.

"No nightmares tonight," he told her.

****

CHAPTER NINE

Dr. Stan Fielding stared at the report that his friend had made for him from the lab, results of tests run on the stone. Just as he had suspected, there was some element that was nothing like anything anyone had ever seen or heard of. Even the computer report listed it as an unknown element.

The stone was still in the small box, sitting on the desk as Stan re-read the report.

Rachel Gwynn, the lab assistant, walked in. She was young, bright, and very beautiful but totally dedicated to her work. She was ambitious and meticulous with her reports and would check and double check her results. She always wore conservative clothing and kept her social life private and away from the lab.

Stan had liked her from the first day she had started, shortly before John had left the lab.

"The old man sent down some more tests for that government project he is trying to get," she said as she walked up to Stan.

"Wonderful," Stan said as if he didn't have enough work to do. "Sometimes, I really wish John had come back."

"I thought that that was who that was yesterday," she said. "Is he coming back?"

"No," Stan confessed, "he just wanted me to look at something."

Rachel found a chair and sat across from Stan.

"Anything interesting?" she asked.

"Just a rock," Stan said without looking up from the report. After a moment, he did look up at her and realized that she had the look of someone that did not believe what they had been told. "I'm completely serious, it is just a small stone that he wanted some tests done on."

"Hey, if that is your story, stick to it," she said with sarcasm.

Without another word, he opened the box and slid it across the desk toward her. For a moment he thought that he saw a strange red glow coming from the stone inside the box and he shuddered briefly.

Rachel pulled up a chair and looked inside the box at the stone. She immediately noticed the three vertical lines that ran perpendicular across the rock. She began to reach for the stone when Stan grabbed her arm making her jump in surprise.

"I just wanted a closer look," Rachel said, pulling her arm from his grip. "What's the big deal, Stan? It's just a rock. It isn't like it is going to jump out of the box and bite me."

"I wouldn't be too sure about that," Stan replied.

"Don't talk in riddles," she continued. "We are both trained scientists. Are you going to tell me that this is some sort of snake rock that bites people?"

Stan felt the wound that he had received from the stone the day before throb in pain. He wanted to tell her about the report that had found the unknown element. He wanted to tell her about the nightmare that he had had the night before where he had killed her. He wanted to tell her about the low almost inaudible voice that seemed to be coming from somewhere deep inside his brain. All of this he so desperately wanted to tell someone, anyone, but his scientifically trained mind tried to find its own answer.

"What is it, Stan?" Rachel asked. "You look pale? Are you getting sick? You didn't eat in the cafeteria again?"

"No, Rachel, I'm ok," he answered. "I suppose that I have been overworking myself since John left."

"Well, that is what I am here for," she said, reclining a little. "Besides, Stan, I thought that maybe you might be getting ideas about me."

Stan had been rubbing his temple when he looked up at her. His brow furrowed as he saw a slight transformation come over Rachel. Her face had seemed to harden and her mouth was larger, disproportionate to the rest of her features. Her teeth looked whiter and sharper, almost as if she were growing fangs.

"Wouldn't you like to rip these clothes off of me," Rachel said, her voice a husky whisper, "spread my legs until they break? Wouldn't you like to eat my pussy, take one of those scalpels and spill my insides onto the floor and bathe in my blood?"

Stan's stomach lurched before he said, "What did you just say?"

He looked again, only to see Rachel, prim and proper sitting on the chair.

"I said," she began slowly, "what are you going to do with the stone?"

"I thought that perhaps I could use the laser," Stan said.

"Oh, right," Rachel said and laughed. "The old man will gladly let you use that thing on some personal project."

"No, Rachel," Stan said and stood up. He walked around the desk and stared at the stone. The red light from within began to glow and pulsate. "I wasn't talking about the stone. I have something much more exciting in mind."

Rachel looked up at her colleague and saw his eyes glowing a faint red. She shivered slightly.

Stan looked away from the stone at Rachel. He smiled.

****

CHAPTER TEN

John was happier than he had ever been. For two straight nights the entire family had gotten some much needed sleep. Bobby was progressing in school to the point where even the incident in the lunchroom with the bully had been forgotten. According to Bobby, the bully was now a friend. April had been working feverishly at her new manuscript and the pages that John had read had confirmed that she still had the talent for creating a chilling story.

Even he had been able to work at some of the projects that he had told Stan that he wanted to do after leaving the lab. He had managed to equip an area of the basement as his own personal laboratory and had begun making copious notations in a book that he hoped would someday out sell his own wife's novels. It was a dream that he had never shared with her. Everything that he had managed to do over the course of two days after leaving the stone with Stan he had been able to do without the help of a drink. At times he had wondered why he had ever started drinking again in the first place. He had not even set foot in the bar in town and all thoughts of buying the place had been replaced with calculations and formulas.

For the first time since moving into the house all was peaceful.

The knock on the door was loud and authoritative. John looked up from the notebook that he had brought from the basement to work on. The knock came again and he managed to place the book aside and rise out of his easy chair, ready to pounce on the inconsiderate intruder who would dare interrupt the peaceful domesticity of his home. April was in her office and Bobby was in his room creating another beautiful work of art.

"Just a second," John yelled out as the knocking became more persistent.

Opening the door with several expletives in mind to unload on the intruder, he was taken aback at the grizzled face with lines of a hard life etched into them. The thinning grey hair was matted with what John assumed was hair oil. The rumpled brown suit and yellow tie did not match and the pot belly that was trying to hide behind an even old raincoat was not succeeding. The soft grey eyes under bushy black eyebrows were the only thing that seemed kind about the man.

"Colombo, I presume," John said.

The man smiled, a winning smile, one that would put anyone at ease immediately. "You wouldn't be too far off, Mr. Tanner?" the man asked.

"Well," John began, "I am John Tanner if that is what you were asking."

Removing a well worn wallet from his inside jacket, he presented his badge and identification card to John, saying, "Detective Stefano."

"You are a little bit out of your jurisdiction, aren't you?" John asked, noticing the Atlanta Police Division emblem.

Placing the wallet back into his pocket, Stefano said, "Well, sometimes our investigations take us almost anywhere. Just last month I had to fly out to California to question a potential witness who had been on vacation. Turned out to be a wasted trip since the person I was sent to interview had passed away after going home. The whole thing could have been handled with a simple phone call but what does my captain say? Stefano, you are going to California for the weekend. Hey, I ask you, Mr. Tanner, what would you have done? Now listen to me, rambling on and on about something that you probably have no interest in."

"I would like to know what a detective from Atlanta is doing standing on my doorstep," John said.

"If you don't mind," Stefano began, "do you think that I could come in for a moment. I promise you that it will only take a small amount of time. I just have a few questions that would help me clear up a case that I was assigned to."

"Please, come in," John said and stepped aside for the portly detective. "Would you like a cup of coffee?"

"Unfortunately I am not allowed to ingest any type of caffeine according to both my wife and my doctor," Stefano said. "I take it with three sugars and two creams, if you don't mind."

Smiling, John led the detective into the kitchen.

"This is really quite a lovely home that you have here," Stefano said. "My wife and I live in a little apartment on the East side, nothing special mind you. My son and his wife live in Oregon where he does forestry work or mows grass; I never can get it straight."

John set the cup of coffee onto the table and motioned for the detective to sit down.

"Now, Detective Stefano, can we get to whatever it is you want to ask of me?" John asked. "How can I help a detective from Atlanta?"

The detective paused, taking a sip of the coffee and nodded his approval. He rummaged around in his pockets and finally found a small notebook. Flipping to a page he said, "Do you know a man by the name of Stan Fielding?"

"Yes," John answered a note of concern in his voice. "We worked together. Why do you ask?"

"I didn't know we had company," April said as she entered the kitchen. Pouring herself a cup of coffee she stood beside John.

"This is Detective Stefano from Atlanta, honey," John said. "This is my wife, April."

"How do you do, detective," April said.

"Please, Mrs. Tanner, I am not Colombo," Stefano said with a grin. "My first name is Harry, not detective. I may look like the squirrely little guy just in bigger proportions."

"Then you must call me April," she said, sipping her coffee.

"April it is," Stefano said. "I was just telling your husband what a beautiful home you have."

"Thank you, Harry," April said and waited. She could tell that the detective was rolling her full name in his head. She had seen the look before from other people that she had met. It was the quizzical glare that always gave it away. The person would sometimes stop in mid sentence, looking her up and down, trying to place the name, knowing that they had heard it or seen it somewhere but could not quite get to the point of full remembering. Then there would be the flash of recognition.

"I have got it!" Harry said and slapped the table. "April Tanner, author of some of the most terrifying novels ever written. My wife has a copy of every one of your books and is always the first in line to buy the next one."

April gave him her winning smile and fell into the celebrity mode that she had adopted over the years when meeting a fan. "Then give me just a moment and I will be right back, detective." April hurried to the basement and picked up a copy of her first novel from a box that held several more. These were the first edition printings and she only gave them to certain people. Once they were gone, there would be no more. Taking a pen from her desk, she signed the front page with a note that read 'to my number one fan', leaving a space for the name.

Joining the others back in the living room, she asked the detective for his wife's name.

"Molly," he told her, smiling broadly.

After the final signature, she handed the book to the detective who carefully took it as if he were holding the Holy Grail. Reading the inscription, he closed the book and read the title.

"I think that she has read this one a hundred times," he said proudly. "She is going to flip when I give it to her."

"You tell her that it is a first edition, not many of them left floating about," April said.

"Now what can we do for you, detective?" John asked again.

"Well," he began, "to be completely honest, I'm just doing some background work for an ongoing investigation. Nothing having to do with either one of you or with your son."

"What sort of investigation?" April asked.

Referring back to his notebook, he asked about Stan again.

"Yes, Harry," April said. "We both know him. John worked at the same lab for, oh, let me see, over ten years, wasn't it?"

"Something like that," John said. "Has something happened to Stan?"

"You might say that," Stefano told them, deadly serious. His entire demeanor changed and he was back in the official capacity of his badge. "I hate to be the one to tell you this, but Mr. Fielding is dead."

April gasped and John felt his lower jaw drop.

"What happened?" John asked. "I mean, was it an accident?"

"That is what we at the station are trying to find out," Stefano answered. "I understand that you went to see Mr. Fielding the other day."

"Yes, I stopped in for a little while," John told him. "I think we went out for lunch."

"Could you tell me the reason for your stopping in to see him on that particular day?" the detective said.

"Sure," John began. "My son had found a rather unusual stone out in the woods when we first looked at the place. I thought that maybe I could get Stan to tell me what sort of minerals made the thing up."

"How was the stone unusual?" Stefano asked.

"Well, it was flat, almost a perfect circle and it had some sort of markings on it that I was sure could not have been made through natural erosion," John explained. "I stopped in and asked Stan if he could run some tests to determine the elements of the stone."

"Was there anything unusual about the outcome of those tests?"

"In a way, I guess you could say that there was," John said and saw the concern in April's eyes. "The computer read out said that there was a slight trace of an unknown element."

"What did you get out of that?"

"Well, as Stan and I had agreed, it could have been something that was not programmed into the computer," John continued. "He asked if he could hang onto the stone for a little while and take it to a friend that worked in another lab across town. They have a much better computer, more up to date."

"I see," Stefano said. "What time did you leave Mr. Fielding?"

"Oh, I guess around two, I really can't be sure exactly what time," John said.

"What exactly happened, Harry?" April asked.

Stefano was silent for a moment, as if weighing certain possibilities in his mind before continuing. He was absolutely certain that neither one of the Tanner's had anything to do with what had happened to the late Stan Fielding. He had already checked security camera's, noting that John had indeed left just before two in the afternoon. He had asked around the town about the Tanner's whereabouts and had discovered that they were the local celebrities, more her than him but he had been highly spoken of by a local tavern owner. Billy, their son, had had a small run in at school but the incident had apparently been forgotten.

After a moment longer, Stefano made up his mind.

"Mr. and Mrs. Tanner," he began, "I am going to have to ask and it is a question that I really don't want to get into but we have to have a complete report. Was there any history of mental illness with Mr. Fielding? I mean, did he ever seek psychiatric help for problems that he was having that you know of?"

"Stan was the most level headed guy that I had ever met or worked with," John said without hesitation. "I know some people make a quick judgment about scientists being a little crazy but that is just a myth. No, Stan never had any sort of mental breakdown during the years that I worked with him."

"Harry, what happened?" April asked again.

"I am about to do something that I have never done in my entire career as an officer or detective," Harry began. "To be honest, everyone, including myself, is completely stumped. Would you two mind coming out to the car with me? I have something that I want to show you, and then perhaps you can rethink the answer to that last question."

With concern, April and John followed Stefano to his non descript Ford. Waiting for him by the back of the car, they watched as he reached into the backseat and rummaged around for an official looking file folder. Joining the couple, he laid the folder on the car without opening it.

"Now, Mrs. Tanner…"

"April, please," she reminded him.

"April," he said with a slight smile, "what I am going to show are the crime scene pictures. They are pretty gruesome. I don't think that even you could come up with something like this for one of your books."

"I understand," she told him and took a deep breath.

Stefano opened the file to the first picture.

Both John and April gasped at the same time.

In most movies and television shows, crime scene pictures are always in black and white. What Stefano revealed was a full color horror show.

John could hardly make out the lab in the picture. The photo was taken from the doorway. Bottles and instruments had been thrown and broken. Different chemicals used for testing were splattered everywhere. Looking closer, he could see the pools of blood on the floor and the streaks on the walls.

"My God," April said.

Stefano slowly turned to the next picture.

April wanted to scream but held back. She looked away momentarily before turning back to see the awful picture.

"Who is it?" John asked.

"She was identified as Rachel Gwynn, a lab assistant," Stefano told him. "Do you think that Stan would have been capable of doing that?"

"No way," John said quickly. "He loved her, I mean as an assistant. They didn't date or anything, although I think that Stan would have wanted to. I can't believe that he would have done such a thing."

The picture showed Rachel, her nude corpse tied at her wrists and ankles, suspended from the ceiling and spread eagle. Where her mid section should have been, just below her blood caked breasts, was a gaping hole. Blood had pooled under the body and her eyes were open in terror. A silent scream held her mouth open. John shuddered slightly as the memory of the nightmare from a few nights ago came flooding back. He could almost see April in the same pose as blood covered him.

"How did he do it?" April asked.

"Wait a second, April," John jumped in. "We don't know that Stan did this, or do we, detective?"

"According to the security tapes, Stan Fielding and Rachel Gwynn were the only ones in the lab at the time. Unless there is another way to get in there, no one came in or out of the building. We have to assume that Fielding did this, although with what the coroner told me after he threw up, I don't believe it either."

"What did the coroner say?" April asked, still looking at the photo.

"He claims that Mr. Fielding did this with his bare hands. No knife wound of any kind could be found. He literally tore the girl open," Stefano told them. "It is the next picture that has all of us puzzled."

Stefano turned the picture over to reveal yet another tableau of horror.

"Is that blood?" John asked.

"No sir," Stefano answered. "That is the girl's intestinal tract. Stan Fielding took the time to disembowel the girl, and then use the organs to spell out that word on the bulletin board. He very carefully pinned the organs to make the word. It must have taken him hours to do."

John and April stared for an interminable amount of time at the gore. The word seemed to expand and grow as they looked.

"Any idea why he would have made the word 'stone' out of the girls intestines?" Stefano asked.

"You still haven't told us what happened with Stan?" John asked.

"You see, sir, that is my other problem," Stefano said, closing the folder, "we can't seem to locate him."

****

CHAPTER ELEVEN

Detective Harry Stefano left his card in case the Tanner's recalled anything that they may remember regarding the missing scientist. He thanked April again for the book and apologized profusely for the photos. He told them that if Stan Fielding happened to contact them to please let him know and contact the local authorities. With a quick handshake, he was gone.

The rest of the day proved to be arduous at best. April could not get the image of Rachel out of her mind. It was too close to the nightmare that she had. Writing was now completely out of the question so she began to busy herself with mundane housework and thinking of something to fix for dinner. John came to her rescue on the latter.

"How about we go out to eat?" John asked her.

"I love you," she said and as a reward gave him a long and slow kiss.

Plans were made and they wound up back at the restaurant and bar. Martin welcomed the couple back and showed them to a table.

"You know, I think that you guys are the best customers I have, so anything that you need, I will get. If you don't like what I cook, I will personally order something from somewhere else, bring it back here and serve you with a smile," Martin told them as he handed them a menu.

The tension of the meeting with the detective had slowly drained away and the entire family felt better. Martin had made an exception for Billy being in the bar since he wasn't serving anything right now.

"You closed the bar down?" John asked.

"Not really," Martin explained. "I just thought that perhaps if I just concentrated on the restaurant part until around 9, then I would open the bar. That way families could come in, eat, enjoy themselves, and then the adults could either come back for a good time or just take the little ones home. Hey, you still interested in buying me out?"

"We haven't really discussed it," John told him which deflated the smile from Martin's face slightly.

"Well, just let me know," Martin said and took their orders before disappearing into the kitchen.

"Do you really want to buy this place?" April asked.

"You going to own a bar, dad?" Billy asked.

"Hey sport, I was only thinking about it, nothing is set in stone," John said.

The word hung in the air like a pendulum and April shuddered slightly.

"Sorry, bad choice of words," John told her.

The food was finally delivered by Martin and the mood changed from somber to relaxed. Even Billy managed to clean his plate of an oversized cheeseburger and potato logs.

After paying the check, the three returned home. Billy announced that he was working on some drawings for school which left his mother and father to cuddle up on the sofa to yet another classic movie.

"Did you hear that?" John asked.

"I didn't hear anything," April told him, her eyes glued to the television.

"I swear I thought I heard something on the porch," John said, no longer watching the movie but looking towards the front door.

"Maybe it was raccoon," she told him.

"A bear?" John asked.

Now April was no longer watching the movie. She could imagine a large and angry grizzly bear busting through the front door and ripping the entire family apart. Using the remote, she turned off the television.

"You don't think that Billy might have gone outside, do you?" April asked.

"One way to find out," John said and made his way to the boy's room.

"Billy?" he called out and opened the door.

Billy was sleeping soundly on his bed. John quietly stepped in and smiled at the sleeping form. He looked over at the desk where his son had been drawing and marveled at the bright colors and the details of the three of them. A family, happy and content, was standing beside the house.

Quietly, John turned off the light and closed the door. Making his way back to the sofa, he sat beside April and told her that Billy was sleeping.

"You're right," he admitted. "Probably some animal that walked across the porch."

"So," April said softly, "do you want to watch the rest of the movie, or do you have something else in mind?" Her hand touched her right breast and began to tease her nipple.

John took her gently into his arms and kissed her deeply. His hands began to caress her, making her groan with excitement. He began to slowly undress his wife, his tongue licking the nape of her neck and earlobe, something that he knew always drove her wild with passion. He fondled her naked breasts before his tongue found her nipple, making small circles around them.

April held onto him, moaning softly, kissing his head. Her hand managed to find his pants and slowly undid them, reaching in and slowly caressing his member. She loved the way that he responded to her touch and could hardly wait for him to be deep inside her, bringing her to an orgasm time and time again. His rhythm was magic and he would manage to hold off his own orgasm until he knew that she was fully satisfied.

His motions were slow, savoring her skin and scent. This was not the frenetic fucking that they had been experiencing, but a true session of making each other feel good on a physical level as well as an emotional one. The act would be the same but now the feelings of completeness would also be present.

The loud bang from the front door stopped everything.

"Now that I heard," April said, pulling on her clothes again.

"Talk about coitus interuptus," John said and managed to zip his pants up again, although the bulge had made that rather difficult. He walked to the front door and turned on the porch light. "If this is a bear, remember that I love you."

"Stop that!" she whispered loudly. "I love you too; now see what the hell it is, I'm fucking horny now!"

Smiling, he carefully opened the door and looked out into the darkness. He strained to see if there was someone or something out on the lawn, something large enough to make such a powerful bang.

"Anyone there?" John called out loudly.

"Why don't you just invite the killer in to have coffee?" April said sarcastically. "I don't think that you have read anything that I have written."

"Hello!" John called again, ignoring the jibes from his wife. "I don't see anything, or hear anything."

"Great," April said. "Now, get your ass in here and fuck me!"

"Sounds like a plan to me," John said and turned toward her. At first, he was puzzled by the horrified look on his wife's face. There was the hint of a scream on her lips as she began pointing at him. Her other hand had reached her mouth to stave off the screech that she was about to make. John first felt the presence behind him before he turned around and screamed himself.

Stan Fielding, covered from head to foot in dried blood, seemed to leap out of the darkness and into the light of the porch. His face was contorted and the fear that was in him pervaded the air. His arms were outstretched as he stumbled into the house toward John.

"Help...me...please," he said before collapsing onto the floor.

"Shouldn't we be calling Harry?"

April was standing behind John as he was busy at the kitchen sink getting a washcloth wet with cold water.

"Yes, dear," he began, "that is exactly what we are going to do.

First, I want to find out what happened."

"He killed the lab assistant and then came here for some ungodly reason," she told him.

Stan had collapsed onto the floor after reaching out for John. It had taken John a few minutes to get Stan onto the sofa and prostrate. After all, this had been his friend for quite a long time. He had already made up his mind to call the detective but first things were first. Something had made the scientist turn into a raving lunatic and John was beginning to wonder if that something had followed him back to his peaceful and happy family.

"I want to find out why, April," John said, squeezing the cloth of excess water. "You knew Stan just as well as I did. What could have driven him to do something like that?"

"I don't know, and I really don't care," April said, following her husband back into the living room.

Both of them stopped cold, looking at the sofa where Stan had been laying only a few moments before.

"Where did he go?" April said. With dawning horror, she raced up the stairs, taking two at a time, to Bobby's room. Busting in she found her son lying on the bed. He was slowly coming out of a deep sleep, rubbing his eyes which sent a wave of relief over his mother.

John called up from the living room.

"He's fine," April yelled back.

"What's going on, mommy?" Bobby asked, rubbing his eyes again.

"It's ok, honey. Go back to sleep."

Bobby was already getting out of the bed and moving past his mother.

"Bobby!" she called to him as he raced down the stairs.

"Hey big guy," John said as Bobby came bounding into the room. "You should really go back upstairs and go to bed."

"But I'm wide awake now dad," Bobby said, stifling a yawn.

"Sure you are," John said with a slight grin.

April came in and smiled. It still begged the question as to where Stan had disappeared to. The answer came only a moment later.

"He said that it belonged to you!" Stan yelled toward the house. He was standing just off the porch, the white light of the porch light creating an unearthly glow around him. The blood which had matted his hair and stained his clothes was a rusty color that seemed to glow. His eyes were wide and scared.

The family had walked to the front door and stood in the doorway, watching the lunatic closely. Bobby inched closer to his mother, his bottom lip trembling slightly.

"Stan," John began, "why don't you come in and we can talk about this."

"You don't know what I did!" Stan said.

"I do know, Stan. A detective came by earlier today. I saw the photos. I just want to know why you did it," John asked.

"She was so pretty, John," Stan said, his voice sounding far off and not much louder than a whisper. "She told me what to do, even after she was dead, she told me what to do. I saw her eyes when she died. She was still talking to me telling me exactly what to do. I didn't want to do it you understand that, don't you? I didn't want to do what I did, but I didn't have a choice, John. Just like you and April and even Bobby! None of you have a fucking choice!"

Stan looked at John, a tear forming in his eye and falling down his cheek. Raising his right hand, he casually tossed something to John who deftly caught the object.

John looked down and opened his hand. His eyes widened and a new found terror began to form in his chest as he looked at the stone in his open palm. He looked back at Stan and in a few moments wished that he hadn't.

"He said that it belonged to you," Stan said again. Reaching into his pocket, he removed the butcher knife.

John and April sat in the living room as local police, fire, and emergency people came in and went out again. A local cop stood nearby them. John wasn't sure if it was for their protection or if they were about to be placed under arrest.

"Mr. and Mrs. Tanner?"

Detective Harry Stefano stood in the doorway wearing the same coat that he had had on earlier in the day.

"I thought that we might meet up again someday under different circumstances," Harry began as he entered the house. "I thought that you were going to call me if Mr. Fielding showed up here?"

"We didn't have a chance," April began. "How could someone do that to themselves?"

"Believe me, Mrs. Tanner, oh, excuse me, April," Stefano began, "I have seen so many things that one could do to the human body that it would fill up volumes of your books. How is your son?"

"Sleeping," John said absently. "The doctor gave him something mild and it put him right out."

"Did he see what happened?" Stefano asked.

"No, thank God," April said. "When I saw Stan take the knife out of his pocket, I grabbed Bobby and ran into the kitchen. I think John was the only one that saw what happened."

Saw what happened? John wished that he could get the image out of his mind. He knew that for as long as he lived, the death of his friend would be forever etched into his memory.

Stefano asked a few more questions before leaving the family to try and pull things together. He asked the local sheriff if they would be about done with the investigation on their end and was told that they were almost finished. The ambulance had already loaded the remains and had left for the morgue. Too many questions were filling his head and his stomach was beginning to hurt.

"Damndest thing that I have ever seen in my thirty years as coroner," Mike Stacy said to Stefano.

"Can a person really do such a thing as that?" Stefano asked.

"Well," Stacy began, "a person can cut his own throat. That takes very little effort to open the artery. This guy on the other hand would have had to have had super human strength. Detective, he not only cut his throat, he almost decapitated himself. As I saw it, he started under his left chin and pulled the knife across his throat. That should have sent him into instant shock."

"I talked to Mr. Tanner," Stefano continued. "He told me that not only did Mr. Fielding cut into his throat but sawed down into the spinal cord. Is that even possible?"

"Not that I am aware of," the coroner told him. "I understand that he was wanted for a murder in your neck of the woods."

"Bad choice of words," Stefano said. "That reminds me, I need to ask Mr. Tanner one more thing."

"Now you sound like Colombo," the coroner said with a smile which got a dirty look from the detective.

Stefano made his way back into the house and found John still sitting on the sofa.

"Mr. Tanner, did anything else happen that you might remember?" Stefano asked.

John thought back. He could see the entire scene in his mind again; April grabbing Bobby and running toward the kitchen, him standing in the doorway ready to protect his family from whatever harm may come from the lunatic that was once his friend. He saw again in his mind, slowed down to almost stillness, Stan tossing the stone to him. He saw the blood spilling from the wound, the head toppling backwards as the arm of Stan continued to saw through bone and tissue before the body finally crumpled to the ground. He saw himself look at the stone again before walking to the other side of the road and throwing deep into the woods as far as he could.

"I can't think of anything, detective," he told Stefano.

"Just as well," the detective said. "Who knows what could have been going through his mind when he spelled out that word on the wall."

John knew, but didn't want to believe it.

****

CHAPTER TWELVE

The nightmare began with Stan slicing into his throat with the knife. The blood, much more than the human body holds, fell like a waterfall down Stan's shirt and onto the ground. The mouth was still working, saying over and over that 'he wants you to have it'.

John found himself standing on the porch, watching the excess blood pooling below the body; Stan's head hung by a small thread of skin, toppled over and lying on his back. The right hand tossed the stone to John and just as before he caught the damned thing.

John began to walk off the porch, sinking into the blood. By the time he got across the yard he was waist deep and moving slower and slower. He threw the stone deep into the woods and walked back to the porch. Turning to look back into the woods, he saw that they were pulsating with a red glow. Above the tree line, over seventy feet tall, he could see the stone growing larger and larger. It seemed to be rolling through the woods, knocking down trees and rolling over them. Slowly and inexorably, it rolled across the blood pond just skimming the surface. As it got closer, John could see the evil eye deep within the stone and the guttural laugh that seemed to fill the entire woods around them.

John woke bathed in sweat. He looked over to make sure that April was all right and found her to be sleeping peacefully. He gently touched her cheek, brushing away a stray hair from her face. Carefully he got out of the bed and made his way to the bathroom. Splashing cold water onto his face he looked at himself in the mirror expecting to see some horrible creature looking back at him. All that the mirror reflected was his normal everyday image.

Trying to walk as quietly as possible, he went to check on Billy. His son was also in a peaceful sleep. Just as he had done with his wife, he lightly brushed a stray hair away from his son's face.

His stomach lurched as part of Billy's cheek came off, exposing muscle and bone. Billy opened one eye which slowly dislodged itself and rolled down onto the bed in front of John who now stood by the bed. A scream was somehow stuck deep within his throat and he felt powerless to move.

"Daddy?" the thing on the bed said as more bits of skin began to slide off of his face. Bone, muscle and sinew were now exposed as the things teeth began to chatter. It reached out to John who finally found the voice to scream.

"John!"

He found himself in his own bed, his wife shaking him and yelling at him to wake up. Something was holding him within the dream and he found that he could not force his eyes to open.

"John!" April shouted again.

Finally and with a great deal of effort John managed to open his eyes and look at his wife. He saw the concern on her face and the compassion. She began to stroke his head consoling him and telling him that it was only a nightmare. He felt her finger touch his cheek and watched as she pulled away from him in horror.

He reached up to his face and felt the blood pouring from the gash on his cheek. He turned and looked into the full length mirror that hung on the door and screamed again. His face seemed to be melting away; bits of skin and bone were falling onto the bed. Behind him in the reflection he could see his wife, not screaming, but laughing hysterically as she began to masturbate.

"John!"

He was immediately awake. His eyes opened at the sound of his wife's voice calling out to him. He slapped his face to make sure that this time it was not just a continuation of the nightmare. He looked at April who was opening the bottle of water that she always kept on the nightstand in case she got thirsty during the night.

Grabbing the bottle he downed the liquid quickly. His breathing was labored and he felt more dehydrated than if he had been working all day in the summer sun.

"Are you all right, babe?" April asked, reaching out to him.

"Don't touch me!" he barked which made her pull back quickly.

"You were having some nightmare," she said.

"I'm not sure if I still am having a nightmare," he muttered.

"What?"

"Nothing, hun," he told her. "I'm sorry; I didn't mean to yell at you."

April slowly put her hand on his. "It's ok, babe, we all have nightmares. If I didn't have any nightmares I wouldn't be as big as a success with my novels, now would I?"

"I guess you're right," John said and smiled at her.

"You are going to have to give me all the details of that one," she told him, sliding next to him and holding him tightly. "Whatever it was, it certainly scared the hell out of you."

"I'm not sure that I can remember it now," John lied to her. He remembered every terrifying moment but would not dare tell her.

"Perhaps it is just as well," she said.

John slid back down and held April closer, not wanting to let go. In a few minutes, she was asleep in his arms. The same could not be said for him.

After an hour of trying, he finally gave up. Looking at the clock which read 3 in the morning, he decided that maybe something light to eat would help him on his journey to a dreamless state. Carefully sliding April off of his arm which only made her turn over, he put on his robe and made his way to the kitchen.

It wasn't until he was halfway through making a ham sandwich with lettuce and tomato that he realized that he had definitely seen something in the living room. It was something that should not have been there and perhaps he had been mistaken when he first walked through.

"Only one way to find out," he told himself aloud.

At first he was almost afraid to walk back and make the discovery. His feet seemed to be rebelling against his will to move. It took a moment, but they started to behave and he slowly walked into the living room.

Apparently his eyes were having the same consternation as his feet, for when he began walking across the floor they seemed to close tightly.

"It isn't there, I know that it isn't there," he said aloud.

Even with his eyes closed, he knew that he was standing in front of the fireplace. With great reluctance, his eyes slowly opened.

"No," he whispered.

The stone that he was sure that he had tossed into the woods was sitting in its usual position on the mantel.

John wanted to scream again and wake up.

"Do you have any books on the history of this county?"

John had dropped Billy off at the school before finding the county library two blocks away. The sequence of events of what was happening to his family was not making any sense to his scientific mind. Since moving into the house there wasn't anything that was making any sense. He had decided to try to look at more unscientific explanations.

The library was actually quite large for such a small town. Two stories tall with books in different sections on both the upper and lower floors, boasting several very comfortable reading stations, it had the look and feel of some ancient castle located somewhere on the outskirts of London. There was a separate room where fifteen computers were ready and waiting for the next client to explore the internet or perhaps write out the next term paper. On the upper landing were rows and rows of audio books. Across from that was a selection of DVD's that could be checked out.

John was actually impressed.

"Yes sir," the young girl behind the main desk answered him. "That section is upstairs and to your left. We actually have quite an extensive collection from local authors as well as historians who have made a study of the area."

"Thank you," he told her.

"If you would like to check something out, you will need a library card," she reminded him.

"No," he said, "I was just interested in a little research."

The girl became a bit conspiratorial and leaned across the desk. In a soft whisper she said, "We aren't supposed to do this but if you want to know something specific about the history of this place, you need to talk to Mr. Chalmers."

"Who is he?" John asked in an equally low whisper.

"Right now, he is the maintenance man here," she said. "He has lived in this county all of his life. As a matter of fact he has fifteen books that were published and are a part of the collection. He would be the one to really talk to."

"Any idea where I might be able to locate him?" John asked.

"Try the garden outside," she said, her smile telling him that she must have a fondness for the gentleman in question. "It is out the rear exit and to your right. It is quite lovely and Mr. Chalmers always keeps it looking so nice."

"Thank you again," John said.

"Cindy," she told him with a smile.

"Thank you, Cindy," John said and began walking toward the back of the library.

She had been right about the garden, John thought to himself. There was a gravel walkway that made its way into a circle with different varieties of shrubs and plants lining the area. In the center was an ornate canopy with benches for resting. Each plant had a small placard that explained what it was.

"Mr. Chalmers?" John called out and saw a man rise up slowly from the farthest point of the walkway. A pair of pruning shears in his hand and a straw hat on his head, he was the caricature of the elderly gardener who took great pride in his work.

"Yes sir?" the old man called out.

John made his way along the path and joined him beside a beautiful array of roses.

"Hard as hell to grow up here but I try," Mr. Chalmers said.

"They look wonderful," John said, studying the flowers.

"What can I do for you?" Chalmers asked.

"My name is John Tanner and I was told that you were the leading historian of the county," John told him.

Chalmers cackled and said, "You must have talked to Cindy."

"That was who told me where to find you, yes," John admitted.

"That girl is a pure romantic," Chalmers said, placing the shears on the ground. "She's always trying to get me to admit that I am really her grandfather and that I will take her away to some magical kingdom where her handsome prince awaits her."

"That bad?" John asked.

"No sir," Chalmers said wiping his brow with kerchief. "that good. She's trying to be a writer and some of the stories that she can tell, well, I don't mind being a part of them."

"Sounds rather interesting," John said.

"I won't say that I'm the leading historian of the library here in this county," Chalmers said. "I have written a lot about the place and I have lived here all of my 82 years. My family goes back further, of course, but some of them moved away. What was it you wanted to know, Mr. Tanner?"

John wasn't exactly sure how to begin this interview but tried as best that he could.

"What do you know about Wilson's Bluff?" John asked.

"Why don't we go over here and sit in the shade, Mr. Tanner," Chalmers said and pointed toward a bench under a large tree. "And please don't call me Mr. Chalmers. It's Ed or Eddie. When someone calls me mister I just want to scream that I am not that goddamn old."

John already liked the man and smiled.

The two men walked to the bench and sat down. Ed Chalmers wiped his brow again and made himself as comfortable as his old bones could muster. He groaned slightly as parts of his body began to adjust to the position. In a moment, he leaned back and turned his head up to the sky.

"It's a beautiful day," Eddie began. "I'm never sure how many more the good Lord is going to give me, so I try and make the most out of every one of them. Sometimes, on days like today, you just have to stop and look around you at all of the amazing things the Creator gave us. I do my best tending this little patch of His world to help people discover the real beauty of this place. Yes sir, it sure is a beautiful day."

"Mr. Chalmers?" John said. "I would really like to know about Wilson's Bluff if you know anything at all."

Eddie looked at John with consternation.

"Young man," Eddie began, "I know more about that place than anybody. My dad took me hunting up there when I was seven years old and for most of my life I went every season. That is until they turned it into some goddamn residential bullshit. Ruined the whole mountain is what they did. That damn fool Chad Kendrick inherited most of the land up there from his father Thaddeus and decided that cute little boxes would be the thing to do."

"I hate to say this, um, Eddie, but I own one of those cute little boxes," John admitted sheepishly.

Eddie looked at John for a moment and then busted out laughing. The laughing was so hard that it brought on a coughing spurt and John was afraid that the old man was about to choke to death.

"Can I get you something?" John asked, patting the old man's back.

"No sir, but you sure did through me for a loop," Eddie said, managing to talk again. "So you bought a house up on Wilson's Bluff. Damn! I didn't think anyone would be fool enough to live up there."

"Well," John began, "it is a nice house."

"Oh, I am sure that it is," Eddie said sarcastically. "So would you like to tell me what is going on inside this nice little house?"

"I'm not sure what you mean," John said.

"Oh come on now," Eddie said looking John full in the eye. "You wouldn't be interested in Wilson's Bluff for the sheer joy of it. I may be old but I'm not stupid. I haven't lost the capacity for rational thinking yet."

John took a deep sigh and began to tell him of some, but not all, of the events. He left out the majority of the bad dreams but included the sudden personality changes that he had noticed from both himself and his wife and child. He also left out the fact that his best friend had committed suicide on his front lawn.

"Well," Eddie said wiping his brow again, "I will tell you a few things. You don't have to worry about there being some ancient Indian burial ground your house is built on. Matter of fact, I don't think anything really bad happened up there in the entire history of the county. Maybe that first family that moved in and perhaps the second one who was killed. There was the accident that happened while your house was being built, but as far as I know, that is the only thing that has happened on that hill."

"You are absolutely positive?" John asked.

Scratching his chin, Eddie thought back.

"Now, wait a minute," Eddie continued. "There was a feller from the University that died up there. You have to remember that this was some time ago. Apparently he killed some student and then took off. His car was found the next day completely burned to a crisp with him in it."

"That happened where the house is?" John asked.

"Well, you said you owned almost five acres of land so I suppose that it could have happened somewhere on that lot."

"Mr. Chalmers!" a high pitched screeching called out.

"Oh shit," Eddie said under his breath.

John looked to where the voice had come from.

She was about five foot seven, plump with obviously died raven black hair that had been curled around her head. She had on enough make up to make any professional clown proud. She was dressed in a flowered print muumuu that could have blinded anyone with its bright colors. She was currently waddling over to the two men.

"Who, or what, is that?" John asked.

In a low voice Eddie answered, "That is Mrs. Alice Richards, miss high and mighty of the town. She has been on every committee that had anything to do with what she calls cultivating the culture of this quaint little village. She is also on the board of directors of this library and has on many occasions made it known that I am no longer needed."

"So she was born here?" John asked which made Eddie laugh.

"Hell no," Eddie began. "Her and her husband moved up here about ten years ago. Her husband passed away shortly after arriving from a heart attack. I say that he died just to get out from under the bitch. I wonder what bug has crawled up her ass today."

The woman approached them as they stood up to greet her.

"Mr. Chalmers," Alice said, "I do believe that you have once again planted the wrong azaleas across the frontage of the library. I gave you specific instructions on what kind that I wanted."

"Yes you did," he replied, "and as I informed you that in this climate they would not grow which is why I planted the ones that are there now."

"Well," she began, puffing out her chest a little to let him know who was in command, "I suggest that next time you go through the landscape committee to make any changes to the plans that have been meticulously drawn out and approved. Do I make myself clear?"

"Words cannot express how much I understand you," Eddie told her which made John grin.

"I deeply apologize sir," Alice Richards said turning to John, "for having to berate an employee." She stuck out her hand to John and said, "I am Mrs. Alice Richards, chairwoman of the library committee for our quaint little village."

John gently shook the woman's hand (like grabbing hold of a snake, he thought to himself), and said, "John Tanner."

"I don't believe that I have seen you before, or have I and have just forgotten," she told him.

"No," he answered, "my family and I moved here just about a couple of weeks ago. We live up on Wilson's Bluff."

"I see," she said, beaming with new found admiration. "That is quite an exclusive area. Tell me, are you famous?"

"Only in my chosen field," John began, "I'm a scientist doing some private work."

"What does your wife do, or is she a stay at home parent?" Alice asked.

"She's a writer," he said, almost regretting saying it. He had forgotten that as soon as people like Mrs. Alice Richards found out who April was, they would want to stop by for tea and cajole her into a personal appearance or lecture, non gratis of course.

"Would I know her?" Alice asked. "That is, would I have been fortunate enough to read anything that she has published?"

"Only if you wanted to have nightmares," John told her.

And there was the look that John had been waiting for. It was the same dawning realization that the detective had given April and him the night before.

"Alice Tanner?" she exclaimed. "You are the husband of one of the most prolific horror authors of our day? Oh, Mr. Tanner, I simply must ask you to see if she would perhaps speak at one of our book club meetings. It would definitely be a feather in my cap if she appeared. Do you think that she would grace us with an appearance sometime?"

"Well," John began, "usually things like that are handled through her agent and publisher. I know that she has been working on a new novel and she gets very busy after it is released."

"Surely she would make the time some Wednesday evening, that is when we meet, right here at the library, since she now lives in our quaint little town. Oh do please ask her," she extolled.

"I tell you what," John said, "why don't you go to the house and simply introduce yourself and tell her that I sent you there." John knew from past experience that April would kill him if the stout woman actually showed up on their doorstep. Something deep down inside him was telling him to do exactly what he was doing, as if some force were driving events surrounding the family. Try as he might he could not resist the voice that was only a whisper inside his mind.

Giving Alice the address, he watched as the waddling lady made her way back inside the library.

"No good busy body bitch," Eddie said which gave John a

chuckle. "Why the hell did you go and do that?"

John, still looking at the area where April had been, said, "I was chosen."

"Chosen? Chosen for what?" Eddie asked perplexed.

John turned to the old man. Smiling, he said, "The wooded area behind the edge of the building, do you tend to that as well?"

Eddie looked to where John was pointing and said, "That's always been called Hush Woods because you can go in there and it is like being in a cathedral. Everyone seems to talk in hushed silence, as if the trees are listening to the secrets being told. There is a sort of natural rest area about a thousand feet in, if you would like to see it. I go in there occasionally to spruce it up a little. I keep telling Mrs. High and Mighty that we need to create a walkway and some signs for people to explore but she always keeps putting me off."

"Let's go see it," John said.

Eddie wasn't quite sure he had seen the soft red glow in John's right eye and had simply put it off as a trick of the light.

The two men moved towards the wooded area with Eddie leading the way. He did not see John pick up the pruning shears from the ground.

****

CHAPTER THIRTEEN

School had been dismissed and Bobby was taking the bus home. Across the aisle was George casting evil glances in Bobby's direction. He still had not forgotten the incident in the lunchroom even though Bobby had tried to make up for it in a number of ways. George had even accepted the caricature that Bobby had done of him as a superhero.

The kick to the groin, however, had never been very far out of George's mind. He had planned ways of getting the little faggot alone, perhaps cutting off his balls and feeding them to him. His imagination had run wild with myriad ways of revenge that involved hot pokers, needles, and knives. He could see in his mind's eye the pleading little boy lying on the ground crying for his mother. Perhaps, George had thought to himself, he would make the faggot watch as George killed his parents before torturing him to death.

All of the ghastly visions caused George to smile.

"Want to come over to my place?"

George looked up and saw the little faggot was actually talking to him and asking him a question.

"Why would I want to go to your place?" George asked in the bully voice that he had adopted years ago.

"Well," Bobby began, "my dad is a scientist who has been working on some really neat stuff. He showed me how to do some experiments with stuff I find around the house, you know like bleach and baking soda and salt."

"That's faggotty shit," George said.

Bobby thought for a moment, listening to the small voice that had been whispering in his mind the entire day, telling him that he had been chosen. For his entire life, he had always been picked last for anything, but the voice was now choosing him for something special. When Bobby asked what that something special was, it would go silent for a while. Eventually, it would begin whispering again, telling him the wonderful plans that it had for Bobby because he had been chosen.

"I can make a bomb," Bobby announced.

Now what made him say that? He didn't know anything about making an explosive. He was strictly forbidden to touch any of his father's work and especially the chemicals that his dad used for experiments. While it was true that his dad had let him help with simple things, Bobby did not have the first inkling on how to make a bomb.

George turned towards the front of the bus and said, "Bullshit."

"I can really," Bobby said. "Nothing like something that would blow up a building, but it sure would do some havoc to a mailbox."

"You are so full of shit, Tanner," George said, although he was beginning to formulate a plan that not only would exact revenge on the little twerp but George would not have to lay a finger on him.

"Ok," Bobby said and turned toward the window. "Have it your way. I'm full of shit."

A few miles went by before George was satisfied with his plan in which Bobby would make a bomb, blow something up, and then George would let the little faggot's parents know as well as the police. George even thought that he might get some kind of reward for turning in a serial bomber. Better to catch a crazy person while they are young and blowing up mailboxes than when they graduate to full scale buildings with people in them.

"You can really make a bomb?" George asked.

Bobby turned, the faint red glow dimming from his left eye, and smiled.

April Tanner was sitting naked on the floor of the living room, her hands caressing her body as she was looking up at the stone that sat once again on the mantel. She had been sure that John had thrown it into the woods but was glad that apparently John had found it and brought it back into the house. She could see the faint red glow deep within, pulsating in a beat that matched the motions of her hands. She tweaked on her nipples hard, making herself wince and moan with both pain and pleasure. Her left hand made its way towards her crotch as if it had an independent will of its own.

The voice inside her head whispered that she had been chosen for something very special as she began to caress herself just above her clitoris. The power that she felt inside her was growing stronger as she began to rub herself harder and harder, bringing the explosive climax that she knew was coming.

The knocking on the door startled her. She looked down at what she was doing and could not remember why she was doing it or even why she was naked. Quickly reaching for her clothes, she dressed and made her way to the front door. Opening it she found herself confronted with what looked like a reject from the Wizard of Oz. The portly woman stuck out her hand in greetings.

"My name is Alice Richards," she introduced herself, "I met your husband at the library just a short time ago. He gave me your address and well, I took it upon myself to come up and see you just as soon as possible. You know, I am probably your number one fan."

Alice swore to herself. Just wait until that husband of mine gets home, she thought. She began concocting all sorts of nastiness that she would perpetrate on his manly jewels for doing this to her.

"Please, come in," April said, stepping aside for Alice.

"You have a very lovely home," Alice said, looking around at the living room.

"Can I offer you something to drink?" April asked trying desperately to think of something to get rid of her. Out of all the plots and monsters that she had invented in her entire career, she was now at a complete loss as to how to get rid of the little troll of a woman.

The voice came into her mind full force. She glanced up at the stone and saw the red pulsating light growing brighter. She looked back at Alice Richards who was oblivious to the stone or the strange light which seemed to be filling the room.

"How about I make some coffee," April said. "John will be home soon and I was just getting ready to start dinner."

"That would be lovely, dear," Alice said with a smile. "Perhaps you could go down and eat my smelly old pussy."

April was startled momentarily and asked Alice to repeat herself.

"I said that it is great to get away from that smelly old library," Alice said with another winning smile.

The two women walked toward the kitchen. April showed her guest where to sit while she busied herself with making coffee. After pouring water into the automatic coffee maker, she turned to look at the back of the old troll's head. The voice inside her mind became louder.

"Are you from here?" April asked.

"Oh no," Alice answered, turning in her chair to face the author. "My husband and I moved up here about ten years ago. He passed away shortly after we moved in, bless his dear soul. I often warned him about his diet of salt and red meat and his drinking, while manageable, was something that he should have stopped. Time and time again I warned him. Did he listen? Well, you know how men are. They think they know everything about everything and we are just the poor old helpless women that need to be taken care of. He passed away, heart failure, and I continued on here making my own life."

"You never met anyone else?"

Alice frowned and said, "He was my first and my last, just as I hope that you and your husband are."

April turned and grabbed two glasses from the cupboard. Taking down the cream and sugar, she opened a drawer to retrieve a spoon for her guest. Just as she was about to reach in, she noticed that she had opened the second drawer where she kept the steak knives and cutting knives. Looking down, she thought that the longest knife was glowing a fiery red. She picked it up and began to run her index finger along the blade, feeling the sharpness without actually cutting herself.

"May I inquire as to the nature of your visit, Mrs. Richards?" Alice asked, still looking at the knife.

"Well, as I have already told you, I am your number one fan," Alice began. "I am the chairwoman and president of the Book Club at the library. We meet every Wednesday evening around eight and have a few snacks with some coffee and discuss books that we are reading and make suggestions for future books to peruse. We have actually done three of your books so far and as I understand from your husband that you are currently working on a new one. I was wondering if it would be at all possible…"

April didn't allow her to finish the sentence, saying, "Would I come down to discuss my approach to writing with your little group. Isn't that what you were going to ask me?" April still had her back turned to the woman, the knife held tightly in her hand. "Yes, you come here to my home with a request that is usually handled through my agent, but of course you didn't take into consideration that this was my home and that perhaps I would like a little privacy? Do you know what I was doing before you so rudely knocked on the door?"

Alice was beginning to get apprehensive. The nice and normal conversation that she thought that she had been having with the well known author had turned very nasty and very quickly.

"I do apologize if I inconvenienced you in any way…" Alice began and started to rise up off the kitchen chair.

April turned, the knife held tight, her eyes glowing red.

"Sit your fat ass down!" she barked.

Alice decided that sitting back down would be the best course of action. She kept her eyes on the knife, carefully calculating the odds of running to the front door and escaping an obviously deranged person. Perhaps writers of horror fiction began to take their work a little too seriously and became candidates for the lunatic asylum. She had never heard about King or Koontz chopping up someone in their kitchen with a large knife. Her fear was rising as she watched April approach her, the knife seemingly three times bigger than before, glowing an odd looking red color. She realized with ever mounting fright that the author's eyes were also glowing the same brilliant color and the entire room, if not the whole house, was bathed in this unearthly glow.

"I was enjoying myself, do you understand?" April began, the knife clutched tighter and tighter. "I was sitting naked on the floor and fucking myself because my useless husband doesn't know anything about the female body! Do you hear me? I was about to have the most satisfying climax of my life when you and your fat, ugly, gut wrenching knock disturbed my concentration! Would you like to taste my pussy on my fingers? You could have had my cum you stupid bitch! You stupid bitch! You stupid bitch!!!"

Alice's mouth opened wide for an ear shattering scream which never came.

April plunged the knife into the gaping mouth, twisting and turning, carving the tongue and throat from the inside. Blood began to spurt onto her chest and smiling face. She released the knife and watched as the body convulsed in its death throes. She took off her clothes and began to bathe in the spurting blood, covering her body with hot fluid. Grabbing the knife, she twisted again and pulled it out along with the woman's two front teeth. She began to stab at the chest over and over again. On the final plunge, she carved her way down the abdomen and to the crotch.

"Hey, did you hear something?"

George had followed Bobby through the front door after getting off the bus. Bobby had laid his book satchel down next to the front door and told George to do the same.

Listening, Bobby said, "I don't hear anything. C'mon, the lab is in the basement." Bobby snickered at what he had just said, thinking that perhaps he should have said 'laboratory' and used the mad scientist voice.

"Is anyone else home?" George asked in a whisper.

With a sigh, Bobby called out, "Mom?"

From the kitchen, April answered, "I'm in the kitchen, Bobby, making dinner. Everything ok?"

"Yea, mom," Bobby answered back and motioned for George to follow him.

As the two boys passed by the fireplace, Bobby glanced up at the stone and could see the small red glowing light deep within. He began to hear the whisper somewhere deep inside his mind and knew that he was the one that had been chosen. George would play a very big part and Bobby was trying to calm his excitement at the prospect of what the voice had told him was going to happen.

"Looks like a bunch of junk to me," George said when the two had made their way to the basement.

Pointing to the desk on the other side of the room, Bobby said, "That's where mom works. I'm not supposed to read anything from there, but sometimes I sneak a peek. Want to see what she's working on?"

"You said you could make a bomb," George reminded him. "So, are you gonna make one or what?"

"I'm getting to it," Bobby said walking behind the table that contained different sizes of test tubes and Bunsen burners. "You have to be careful when you do this or you might wind up blowing your face apart. Why don't you sit in that chair and make yourself comfortable while I get what I need."

"You sure you know what you are doing?" George asked a little more nervously than he had intended.

"Look," Bobby said, walking back around and standing toe to toe with the bully, "do you want to go and blow something up or don't you?"

"Sure I do!"

"Then shut your pie hole, sit down, and let me get to work. It isn't magic you know."

George sat down and watched as Bobby walked to the other end of the basement, disappearing into the darkened corners. He stared as long as he could, thinking that he could see the faggot moving around, looking for possible ingredients. He heard tinkling of glass and other objects being moved around and thought that perhaps he should just forget the whole thing and go home.

"Hey, Bobby, you there?" George called out.

George thought that he saw something moving in the darkness. He stared more intently and was caught off guard by the can of soup that came flying out and knocking him between the eyes. A veil of nausea swept over him and as he looked, he swore that he could see two Bobby's running toward him with a baseball bat. Trying to fend off the attacker, he felt the bat connect with his temple.

Everything went black for George.

****

CHAPTER FOURTEEN

John had been driving around for hours, circling the town, watching the people coming and going. He sat at the small town park, gazing at the waterfall that had been built as a centerpiece. He watched the colors of the water change with the refraction of the sunlight and felt completely at peace.

He had been lucky that he had found the old t-shirt and jeans that he had left in the car. The blood from Mr. Eddie Chalmers had made a complete mess of his other clothes. He had spent a considerable amount of time at the clearing with the old man. He thought that Stan must have felt the same way while pulling out the intestinal track and spelling out the word 'stone'. He left Chalmers lying beside the gore, his chest cavity torn open and the pruning shears stabbed into the forehead.

John reached over onto the passenger seat and patted the prize that he had neatly wrapped up in his old shirt. The blood had congealed and looked more like rust. He smiled and waited for the voice inside to tell him what a good job that he had done. After all, he thought, I am the chosen one.

Twilight had come as John pulled the car into the driveway. Turning off the headlights, he sat in the car, trying to figure out how to inform his family that they must also be sacrificed. He played over and over in his mind what the voice had instructed him to do. It would be so neat and simple that John laughed about the whole thing. There would be hardly any planning, except to inform April and Bobby exactly what he would have to do. Yes, he thought, he would make it seem like a great big joke, a simple practical joke on his family that would end in their demise.

He looked at the house and realized that all of the lights were off except for what seemed to be a soft glow. He wondered if perhaps there had been a power outage, or perhaps April had something truly special in mind. He thought that perhaps one last fuck would be in order before decapitating her. Maybe, he thought, he would kill her while deep inside of her, letting the blood flow over both of their bodies as he pushed deeper and deeper inside of her. He wondered if she would also have an orgasm while the blade of the knife sliced into her throat and through her neck into her spinal cord. There would be no way that she would be able to let him know except for the tightening of her groin around him.

He found himself aroused at the sheer prospect.

Picking up his package, he made his way to the front door of the house.

"Hello, dear," April said as the front door opened.

She was standing at the head of the table that she had set up. All of the good china and dinnerware were spread out neatly, along with decorative cloth napkins. Candles seemed to be lit everywhere in the house. Two candelabra's sat on the table and fixed between them was the dinner that April had so lovingly and with patience prepared.

What was left of Mrs. Alice Richards lay prostrate, her chest opened wide. Sitting in the middle of the cavity was her head, her mouth opened in a perpetual scream, her eyes showing the fright that she felt when her life left her. Her arms and legs had also been removed and now lay in the kitchen sink to be disposed of later that evening.

"It is something very special that I have prepared since something very special is happening tonight," April said.

"Yes, something special," John said, remembering the sexual fantasy that he had just had.

"What do you think?" April asked.

"Where is Bobby?" John asked her.

"He will be up from the basement shortly," April told him. "He has a friend with him. I thought that we could make this a wonderful evening. So, answer my question. What do you think?"

"I think," John began, "that it all looks great. You even look great."

John noticed that she was wearing the short miniskirt that always drove him wild. The white blouse was unbuttoned halfway, revealing part of her breasts. Her face was made up perfectly, as if they were getting ready to spend a night on the town.

"Would you like to fuck me before dinner?" April asked. She bent over seductively looking at him, showing more of her cleavage. Her hand slid the skirt upwards, inviting him to take her.

No, John thought. This was not the way that the voice had planned it and John wanted to go strictly by the plan. He had made all of the arrangements in his mind and knew exactly what he wanted to do and what the voice had told him to do. For the first time since entering his home, he was distracted.

"C'mon, lover," she cooed, "take my sweet pussy and ram your hard cock into it, now." Her breath was coming out in short bursts as her fingers found her wetness, exciting her more.

John looked over and saw the stone. It still sat on the mantel, but the glowing red was now more brilliant ever, as if it were gaining power in ever increasing doses. It seemed to be breathing now, expanding like the chest of a human.

"No," John finally said, "I have been chosen!"

April stood up suddenly, straightening her skirt and buttoning up her blouse. Her entire demeanor changed from seductress to demon.

"Fuck you, John!" she screamed. "He chose me, or didn't you get the memo! Don't you see what I did for him? How long it took to carve into the flesh of this waste of space and prepare such a delightful dinner?"

"Oh, you think that it was a fucking chore?" John asked, his own voice rising in anger. "I was completely out in the open! All I had was a pair of fucking pruning shears and do you have any idea how long it takes to spell out a word with intestines? Stan would know, but he had had stick pins. Halfway through I had to fight with birds who were already circling around. To be honest, I am surprised that no one caught me."

Taking the package from under his arm, he carefully unfolded it to reveal the human heart from Mr. Chalmers. He stroked it like a secret lover.

"Do you see, bitch!" John shouted. "Do you see what I brought to him? He told me that I was the chosen one! Me! Not you! All of my planning on the way back here has now been shot to hell because you think that he has been talking to you!"

"He has been talking to me!" she screamed. "I gave him my body and my soul! He chose me!"

April picked up the carving knife from the table and began to run towards John with it raised. She was ready to make a death swing at his head.

"You're both wrong!" Bobby said from the doorway of the basement.

April and John turned towards their son. The entire room was now glowing red far and above the candlelight. The breathing of the stone was now audible to all of them.

"I was chosen," Bobby said softly. "I think that you both need to come downstairs."

April and John stood in the middle of the basement, seeing what their ten year old son had done. Bobby was smiling and giggling as he danced around his parents.

"Do you see?" Bobby asked with glee. "The voice told me exactly what to do and you know how well I follow instructions. Knock the kid out, tie him up, and then pour those chemicals together in that small jar. I had to make sure that there was a wick to light the fuse, of course. He told me everything and now, you two are to be witnesses to my sacrifice. I am the chosen one!"

"What chemicals did you use, Bobby?" John said in a sober tone. Sober for the first time in days, he realized that something was very wrong. The voice was no longer whispering to him. He could tell that it was no longer there and perhaps he had simply been a pawn in a deadly game that had begun in Hell so many eons ago.

"Just the ones that he told me to use, daddy," Bobby said in a mean tone. "You really aren't as smart as you think that you are. I was the first one that He found, remember? I brought you the stone which means that I had had first contact with it. I have always been the chosen one. After I'm done with Georgie Porgy here, I get to deal with you two!"

Now even April had begun to realize that something was terribly wrong. She could also no longer hear the whispering deep inside her. Nausea had begun to fill her stomach and she wanted to run to her son and take the entire family far away.

"Let's party," Bobby said and lit the fuse.

George, tied to a chair in the middle of the room found his mouth filled with some sort of glass bottle. It had been securely taped around his head. Looking down, he watched as Bobby lit the short fuse and began to try and shake it loose from whatever was in his mouth. The bright flickering flame crept up the string, higher and higher.

"I told you I could make a bomb," Bobby said to George.

"Run," John whispered to April.

"What?" April asked, watching in frightening fascination at the fuse.

"Run," John said louder.

"What about you?" April asked apprehensively.

John turned to his wife, grabbed her shoulders and pushed her toward the stairs. "Goddamnit, run!"

Bobby yelled, "You won't get away, you fucking bitch! We are all going up, except me!"

Bobby began to run past his father but didn't get far. John tripped him and jumped onto his back, pinning him to the floor.

"John!" April yelled.

"Run!" John yelled up to her.

"Daddy, no!" Bobby cried, struggling under the weight of his father.

April ran up the stairs, closed and locked the door to the basement and ran into the living room. She turned and saw the stone, the bright red light pulsating faster. She looked harder and could see the stone changing shape. She could see the diamond shaped eyes beginning to form, the cruel lips that began to smile showing sharpened rows of teeth. The stone seemed to be breathing faster and faster.

From the basement door, she could hear pounding.

"Mommy, please, let me out!" Bobby yelled from behind the door.

"Run, April," John said from somewhere far away, barely audible from downstairs.

April ran out the front door, stumbling in the grass. She lay there for only a moment before looking back at the house.

The explosion began in the basement. The chemicals splattered everywhere and instantly ignited. Within a moment, the entire house was engulfed in flames. April swore that she heard the screams of her husband and son as they were burned alive.

She began to laugh maniacally.

****

CHAPTER FIFTEEN

"Remarkable, truly remarkable."

Dr. Peter Franklin sat behind his oak desk. He turned off the recording that had been made early that morning. He sat back in his leather chair, folded his hands together and looked at his colleague who had been listening, hanging onto every word.

"You say that she has been giving you this same story for how long?" Dr. Sean Kunis asked.

"For the last five years, Doctor," Franklin told him.

"It is one of the most fascinating cases that I have ever run across," Kunis said.

"It is also the reason that I wanted you to hear the recording from this morning. I have tapes going all the back to the time when she first arrived. They are all pretty much the same," Franklin told him. "I wanted you to have a clear picture of her case before you took her to the institute."

"I can see now why you called me," Kunis said. "It is my understanding that you have had no success in treating her psychosis?"

"None whatsoever," Franklin said. "That was why I called you. I have read the articles that you have written on your treatments and the success that you have had. I thought that this particular case might be right up your alley. Besides, after five years I think that maybe some other form of treatment is in order."

"I would like to hear your side of things before I make any sort of decision," Dr. Kunis said. "I read the reports that you sent me last week but I would like to hear about the case in person. Sometimes the way a person speaks about something rather than writing it will give a whole new meaning and perception."

"I agree," Dr. Franklin said and began his story.

"Five years ago April Tanner moved into a house where she claimed to be writing a novel. She says that along with her husband and ten year old boy, they were quite happy. Her son, Bobby, found a stone and it became a sort of talisman for the home to ward off evil spirits. Only something within the stone took over and made them all commit atrocious acts of violence and murder. The house apparently burned to the ground with her husband and son still inside along with the remains of two other victims. She was found on the front lawn by neighbors. After being sedated by local EMT's she was taken to the hospital for observation. When she told her story to the sheriff, he had her committed here. Her story has not changed in five years."

"I am assuming that you did some investigation of your own," Dr. Kunis asked.

Franklin sighed heavily. "After a week of her being here and me having consultations with her, I took a drive to the town and yes it really does exist, as well as a place called Wilson's Bluff."

"What did you find?" Kunis asked.

"Absolutely nothing," Franklin said. "The house she claims to have been destroyed was still standing. The real estate agent allowed me to walk in. I found a cot, a small table with a laptop computer, a little food in the refrigerator, a few utensils in the drawers, and nothing else. I then traced Miss Tanner back to just before she moved into the house."

"What did you find?" Kunis asked, now more interested than before.

"Miss April Tanner, age 38, never married, has been working at the public library in Atlanta for the past 18 years. When I talked to some of her co-workers they told me that she never dated, or at least if she did they never heard about it. She kept to herself and never bothered anyone. She spent most of her time arranging books or reading them. When I looked at her check out records I found that she mostly read horror and mystery novels and short stories."

"Where did she live in Atlanta?" Kunis asked.

"A small apartment on the West side," Franklin said. "I spoke to her neighbors there. They rarely saw her and she never bothered them. I suppose that she was just one of those people who are seemingly made of glass. They don't bother anyone so no one bothers them."

"Remarkable," Kunis said again. "Yes, I would say that it is one of the strangest cases of psychosis that I have ever run across."

Franklin hesitated for a moment and Dr. Kunis could sense that there was something more to the story.

"When I checked around the town, no one noticed her there, either," Franklin said. "She would get a few groceries but then never leave the house. There were never any murders and there was never a Stan Fielding who committed suicide on the front lawn."

"What about the stories of the history of the house?" Kunis asked. "Were there ever any accidents associated with the house or surrounding acreage?"

"Apparently that part of her story is true," Franklin told him. "There are a few more things that I should tell you."

"By all means," Kunis urged.

"Every day, Miss Tanner writes out this story, on paper and hands it to one of the nurses to mail to her publisher. I have taken on that role, in her mind anyway. I have an entire cabinet full of these writings. I think that I should show them to you."

"I would be very interested," Kunis said and watched as Dr. Franklin rose up from the desk and walked to a four tier cabinet. He saw the doctor open a drawer and retrieve a sheaf of paper.

"Tell me what your impression is," Franklin said, handing the doctor the papers.

"This is what she writes, everyday?" Kunis asked, his face frowning.

"Every day," Franklin told him.

"It's the same word, over and over again, on both sides, on every page," Kunis said, looking down again at the one word.

"That's right," Franklin said. "The word 'stone'."

"I take it that she has no family at all?" Kunis said.

"Her parents were killed when she was eight and she was

raised in foster care, having no siblings or any other family," Franklin said. "She spent her entire life alone. There was no husband, no ten year old boy named Bobby, no one else associated with the story that she recites twice a week for me except in her mind."

Laying the paper onto the desk, Dr. Kunis sat back in his chair and said, "I believe that we may be able to help her."

"There is one other thing that I haven't told you," Franklin said. Opening his desk drawer, he removed a small box. With the careful patience of a surgeon, he removed the top and slid the box across to Dr. Kunis.

Putting on his glasses, Dr. Kunis looked down. His eyes widened in surprise as he saw what was in the box.

"Are you telling me..." Dr. Kunis began.

"When I made a tour of the house," Franklin interrupted, "I would swear to you that I did not see it until after I was getting ready to leave. I had just come up from the basement area and was heading toward the front door when I thought that I heard something behind me. I thought that it was perhaps the house settling where I had been walking. I found that sitting on the mantel. I took out my handkerchief, used my pen to scoop it up with and into the cloth, then carefully tied it. Please don't ask me why I didn't dare touch it. I'm not suffering from some form of psychosis of my own or transferring Miss Tanner's own beliefs to mine. I just thought that perhaps I shouldn't handle the thing."

"The stone," Kunis said, "from the story. You are telling me that this is the stone from the story?"

"I really don't know," Franklin admitted. "Perhaps it is, perhaps it isn't. I found it to be a very strange coincidence."

"Then treatment for the psychosis should be very simple," Kunis said. "Simply show her the stone."

"I have sat here behind this desk for the last five years with that box in my desk drawer thinking the exact same thing," Franklin said. "I have also been thinking about the details of the story and the relationship to the stone that Miss Tanner obviously has. I have wondered if showing her the stone would either snap her back to reality or drive her further into her obsession."

"What you are saying is that if she sees the stone, she may follow through and begin to display homicidal tendencies," Kunis said.

"Which is why I contacted you," Dr. Franklin said. "I believe that someone with your experience would fare better than I would. We run a simple facility and yours, in my opinion, would be better suited."

"I completely agree," Kunis said, rising up from the chair and shaking his colleagues hand with a firm grip. "We can make arrangements for transfer in the morning."

"I do hope that you will respect her psychosis of being a publisher," Franklin said.

"Yes, we know how to handle this," Kunis said, looking down at the stone again. "I would ask, could I have that?"

"The stone?" Franklin asked. "Yes, of course."

Dr. Sean Kunis lifted the box and shook out the stone into his other hand. He winced slightly as the stone hit his hand. It was as if something had bit him. Examining his hand, he noticed the small drop of blood that had formed. Wiping it away quickly, he placed the stone into his coat pocket.

"I hope that you will be comfortable here," Dr. Kunis said.

April Tanner looked around the furnished room. It was not like any asylum that had been described in many of the books that she had read. Oh yes, she knew where she was, she just didn't know why.

The room was immaculately done in an oak finish. A comfortable bed sat in the middle and there was a small sitting area by the window which was barred and electrically closed. At least she would be able to see the garden which was directly across from her room. The bathroom, complete with tub and shower was just to the right of the window. A small table beside her bed contained a lamp and a panic button. Except for the location, she thought that perhaps this room was not unlike that of a first class hotel room.

"I'm sure that I will be, Mr. Kunis," April said as she looked around. "So, you will be my new publisher?"

"That is correct, Miss Tanner," Kunis said.

"I hope that we sell a lot of my books," she told him. "I've been working on my twenty second novel. Perhaps Mr. Franklin told you about it?"

"He did indeed, Miss Tanner."

"By the way, it's Mrs. Tanner," she corrected him. "I'm really surprised that my husband and my son, Bobby, have not come to see me. He is a rather brilliant scientist so he is probably working on some top secret chemical for the new space program. Bobby, let me see, he would be fifteen now. A wonderful artist, he is probably having a show at a gallery in New York now."

Dr. Kunis only smiled. His hand was in his pocket, the stone twirling between his fingers. He could almost feel the warmth of the glow from somewhere deep within the stone.

"Well, if there isn't anything else, Mr. Kunis, I would like to get some rest," she said as she sat on the bed.

"There is one thing, Mrs. Tanner," Dr. Kunis told her.

She watched as he walked towards the door which had been left open. He closed it slowly and turned back to her.

The stone in his pocket seemed to be breathing.

Smiling, Dr. Sean Kunis gripped the stone tightly inside his pocket.

"I have something to show you," Dr. Kunis said, his voice deeper and more menacing.

For a moment, April Tanner thought that she could see a faint glow of a red light deep within his eyes.

****

Epilogue

The butler did it.

****

Afterword

Welcome to the other side.

There is no underlying factor or moral to this story, suffice it to say it was simply a horror story based on a very bad dream. I will leave it up to you, dear reader, to find some sense to what you have just read.

I would like to take this particular portion and thank the people who have helped me to continue to write, even though there were times when I was ready to give up. I will not mention any names for fear that I may forget someone and possibly lose a good friend. They know who they are and I gladly dedicate this, my 13th book, (and how appropriate is that) to them.

Thank you, dear reader, for choosing this book as fodder for your nightmares. I hope that I have caused many of them.

Until we meet again, good night, and…

Sleep well.

####

Made in the USA
Columbia, SC
31 July 2021